Not Another Hero

An MM Romance in Space

by

Wendy Rathbone

**Not Another Hero – MM Romance in Space
Copyright © 2019 by Wendy Rathbone and Eye
Scry Publications.**

**A publication by:
Eye Scry Publications**
http://www.eyescrypublications.com

ISBN:
TITLE: Not Another Hero – An MM Romance in Space
Author: Wendy Rathbone
Cover by: Wendy Rathbone

For Della

Always my hero.

Chapter One

The Powers That Be (PTB) used to send technicians into space and an occasional scientist. All that came of it were boring lectures and the ability to repair busted satellites. Financing for further space travel was slow to come. But they fixed that eighty years ago. Now they send Heroes.

The definition of a Hero is less flattering than the generic term. We're glorified porn stars. Actors sent out here with a space opera script of mostly sex scenes. We are filmed twenty-four/seven. We're expendable, we're highly sexed, and we're stupid. Most of us are failed artists with nothing left to lose. As well as an actor, I am a lazy, bad poet who loves to gaze into space. Who better to send off to other worlds? With us, there is the element of sexy drama without the fear of losing some mind valuable to society.

When the PTB signed me up I'd been doing mostly summer stock Shakespeare for no pay. I was a nerdy actor but with a pretty face and managed some good reviews. By some miracle the PTB liked my audition for them and hired me. They changed my name from Weldon Philbert to Stirling Kane, paid for a trip to the most famous flesh-carving institute, Scat Fat, where forty pounds of excess flab was removed in order to make my body lean and perfect, and bought me a whole new Spandex and pleather wardrobe. PTB promised to publish all the bad poetry I wrote out there in space if I turned out to be worthy entertainment.

Now, with twenty-five years of experience and fifty-three missions behind me, I still look like I'm in my mid-twenties and I'm famous. I command my own ship, and everyone who works for me is a Hero, too.

Lacrosse, my ship, houses eight. I sit at her helm and don't do much, since everything is auto-computerized these days. I stare a lot at the stars with a pensive gaze. It's a part of my job, and I'm paid very well for it, thank you.

This mission, we're off to Jupiter for hydrogen samples and I can think of no ship better qualified than mine for the task. Since Jupiter has no solid surface, we won't be landing. But then, you knew that. It doesn't take a scientist to understand those dynamics.

Though fifteen other missions have probed that stormy world, no one has ever gone as close to the planet as we will. Our low altitude probe, complete with diamond-headed bore, is supposed to dive deeper and faster than any other. If it hits solid mass, it will drill. Compressed hydrogen, I'm told by the computer, can be a bitch. Beneath that, someone in the PTB department is hoping to hit rock, and subsequently strike it rich. Diamonds, maybe? Hiding there since the beginning, when our solar system stirred and flared?

"I doubt it," Danielle Blacque tells me when I pose the theory to her over lunch.

I blink and lean forward dramatically. I can't help but flirt with her. Not only is it in this voyage's job description to do so – the more sex we have on these trips, the more recordings of our journey the PTB can sell to the masses – I love sex almost as much as the stars. Unfortunately, she appears not to be interested in anyone but her brother, Drac, who happens to interest me more, actually, but it's only been a week in space so far and I'm trying to save the best for last. He's *that* hot.

"There's nothing but iron in the center of that planet, if there's anything," she replies, ducking her head to avoid my kiss. She pokes at the damp mash on her plate. After all these years of advancements, human beings still cannot make decent fare for long-voyaging that doesn't look like tie-dyed toothpaste. We have the ingredients to cook, and sometimes I do. But most of us are pretty damned lazy.

"How do you know?" I ask.

"Because I read up on it." Her pale blue eyes roll, the long lashes shadowing her cheeks. "Unlike some Heroes, I *can* read, you know."

"Oh. Of course."

"This mission is just a waste of time and money," she adds out of the corner of her beautiful mouth.

"Never!" I argue, pretending to stare hungrily at her breasts through the sheer, red silks of her brassiere.

Don't judge me. This is in the script. I'm supposed to be a dick and pressure her for sex. I'm supposed to leer at big breasts and tight asses, at bulging crotches and flexed muscles.

Danielle is wearing designer PTB red lace leggings, that red top, and nothing more. She looks about twenty-one. She's actually in her late thirties.

"Our missions are never a waste," I tell her.

"I know. I know, we do it for the love of the stars," she says.

"You sound like you're becoming disillusioned."

She shrugs. It's cute. Even though I prefer men, we're all bisexual in this script. I'm a method actor through and through. Who am I to deny a great body?

My groin tightens against my tight leather bodysuit.

"Maybe I am," she says.

She gives no indication she's interested in me. Sometimes it takes time to settle in on a new voyage. To be comfortable with your fellow holo stars. But it's hard not to feel a tad dejected.

When she leaves I sit for awhile and stare at the sloping, silver bulkheads.

This is going to be a long four months.

Chapter Two

In the playroom I lose myself in a holo, a live-mystery simulation.

A young boy on a Martian satellite colony has just been murdered. It's my job to chase down the suspects. I have too many choices to keep track of, and my attention span has always been short, one of the reasons I became a poet and not a novelist. But it's fun anyway.

I get easily side-tracked by virtual hot fudge sundaes and a willowy young man born in space whose heart would burst if he ever set foot on Earth. He may or may not be a suspect. I don't really care because at this point I'm aroused and I'd much rather fuck than solve a mystery.

He's like a bird in my arms, naked and willing, his bones brittle and light. The half-grav of the satellite is almost too much for him as my body pushes his against the velvet cover of his bunk. He's a rarity, now that the new ships have their own Earth-like artificial gravities, and a sweet tenderness wells that I've never felt before.

In this sim, one of the most advanced I've seen, not only can you taste the hot fudge on the sundaes, you can smell people. This man smells like rain and wind, tart on my lips everywhere I kiss him. He has a thin, strong cock, hard as stone against his stomach, and I can even feel the dampness at its head where I press my thumb. I imagine it will taste of rain as well, and I am eager to find out as I rub my palm against his smooth-as-marble shaft.

Just as I get to the point of wishing away my own clothes, wanting to feel him against me skin to skin, the computer image wavers and freezes.

"You have failed to track the next clue in the time allotted," a whispery, androgynous voice states from beyond the frozen scene. The beautiful man in my arms shimmers, a warm mirage fading to clear air. "Nod for retry. Tilt left for abort."

After failure to flirt with Danielle, and now, having just wasted two hours of sleuthing only to have my hard work wiped from memory, I am feeling none too rational. I neither nod nor tilt. Fuck this game! Fuck the computer's commands.

This is the second time this game has done this to me. I rip off the headset and fling it across the room. It hits Armstrong Vaughn hard in the crotch. I didn't even know he'd entered the playroom.

"Oops." I slide out of the sim-chair just as he's removing his own headband. He stares at me, dark brows meeting in a frown.

"What?" he says, picking up my unit from his lap. "You mad at me?"

"Sorry, I thought I was alone. It just flew right out of my hands."

"Well, Captain, I think you're taking these games a little too seriously." His voice is deep, like chamber music.

"There are only three things I take seriously."

"Me, too." White teeth flash against dark pink lips. "The stars, life, and…"

"Want to discuss it further in my quarters?"

"You *are* desperate," he replies.

He's right. I've been horny for hours. And honestly, I've been doing all I can to distract myself from thoughts of Drac. Unreachable Drac. Drac who rarely leaves his quarters.

He's the one I want, and the script is very mysterious about him. We have a lot of leeway in our scripts to ad-lib. The script gives us suggestions for hook-ups and drama, but we are allowed to switch things up, exchange roles if we so desire, and add our own dramas. We're pros, so it's pretty much up to us to give a good show. We are all famous for our performances, so there is no question we'll be fine.

But Drac is new. And I want to conquer that greenie so badly I can taste it.

This is going to be a slow-burn, damn him to Hell. I can tell. But all right, then. I can be patient.

Armstrong gets up from his chair and follows me into the ship's corridor where the hum of the engines is like a soft purr. I love the sound.

All frustrations aside, I absolutely one-hundred percent love my job.

*

Armstrong Vaughn takes me into his mouth with a powerful, wet suction. I've had sex with him three times on this voyage already, and he's always a lot of fun. But my thoughts are on Drac as my fingers weave through his many, tiny braids.

My cock is so hard and his mouth is so hot. I thrust up. He lets me, taking me deep into his throat. Gods, it's good.

I pull out leaving just the tip against his lips and catch my breath. Then I thrust again. He goes with my rhythm. He knows I am trying to make this last, but he is relentless with the sucking. My whole body tingles.

"Wait!" I gasp and pull out. Again, my cock touches just his lips. The bastard sneaks his tongue out and wiggles it against my slit.

I feel a surge of pleasure.

"Damn it! Fuck! You didn't just do that!"

When I push back into his mouth, my cock swells. Nothing can stop it now. I am bursting. I come in sweet throbs, filling his mouth.

He swallows, licking his lips after, then frowns at me. "You are so critical in bed," he complains.

"What?"

"You didn't like what I did?"

I chuckle and smack him on the flank. "I loved it!"

"What?" He bats his eyes. "This?" And he leans down and licks the head of my cock.

I smack him again. "Give me a minute, will you?"

We don't age fast in space. We're all between thirty and fifty, but still young, still with the uncontainable energy of twenty-year olds. When we need them, we get the surgeries and the drugs that keep us virile and horny.

But with all that I still need a break between orgasms. I never got the enhancement that enables multiples because there were too many side effects I didn't like, one being neuropathy of the genitals. Five percent of men get that from the procedure. That means your cock burns. All the time. Possibly for the rest of your life.

No thank you. Not necessary. I'll just drink a bottle of water and doze for five minutes, then I'm good to go again. I've always had a naturally high libido anyway.

While I'm recuperating from my powerful orgasm, I suck on Armstrong's cock. It's longer and fatter than mine, but I'm not jealous. We're all different. I like his cock, but mine's fine, too.

I can only get my mouth half-way down his length, but he is used to that. There really isn't anyone who can take the whole thing into their mouth. It's just too big.

I slobber on it for awhile; it's like candy to me. He tastes spicy, earthy. Like a little piece of home in space.

He makes a lot of noise, moaning and groaning, moving his hips. That and the purr of the air processors in the bulkheads are like security to me. I'm where I want to be. He's enjoying himself quite well, but he doesn't come.

And I know why.

He's waiting for me to come round again. He wants to be fucked.

Well, I can handle that.

I'm hard again. He's beautiful, and having my mouth on him is lovely. My cock wants to play again.

I moved off him and sit back.

With bright, brown eyes he sees my shaft bobbing up. He grins. "Ready?" he asks.

Hell, yeah. I am.

Without any urging from me, he turns over and sticks his ass up. So pretty and tight, the brown skin gleaming.

I grab the lube and play with him, making sure I get it everywhere, even on his balls. He loves that. And I think: *Would Drac love that?*

Damn, I cannot get that dude off my mind.

My fingers find their way inside Armstrong and he hisses "yes" over and over as I stretch him. My forefinger finds that wonderful, internal spongy bump within and strokes. I press a little harder.

Armstrong gives a little yell. I reach around to feel his hard cock swelling.

"It's time," I say. "You ready for a pounding?"

"Please please! Do it hard. Fast and hard. I want to feel you sliding in and out as fast as you can. I want to feel your hips slam my ass."

He's like that. So verbal. His approval rating is high. His fans are screamers themselves.

I'm good in bed. Not to brag. I wouldn't be here if I wasn't. But I'm not into the really rough stuff. Still, I can accommodate this fellow just fine. I love to piston fuck a willing hole.

I add another dollop of lube, then press the head of my cock against him. He's more than ready. He's eager. He pushes back against me and my cock head pops through the tight ring of his stretched hole.

After that, I slide in easily, especially since he's helping a lot by pushing back fast.

He starts his yelling. "Oh, oh, oh!"

I grab his hips for balance, stroke in and out of him once, twice… just to get a feel. Then when I am ready I speed things up.

His voice encourages me.

I press against him, then pull out.

I should probably explain at this point that everything we do on this ship is filmed. There are little nano-bot cameras everywhere. Embedded in the floor, in the furniture, in the bulkheads and ceilings. We even have them in our eyes. We can turn those off, though, for sleep or using the head. Three rapid blinks and they go off. Three more and they're on again.

I pull out and stare at my cock just to make sure the fans get a good look. It's dripping and super hard. I'm a proud man, so sue me.

I plunge back into Armstrong's waiting heat. He tightens around me on purpose.

"Bastard," I grunt.

"Critic," he banters back.

Now I'm ready to rev things up. My thigh muscles flex as I fuck faster. I picture the jiggle of my tight ass, the concave flex at the sides as I take him over and over. Every muscle in me is taught. I hope it's pretty and the lighting is good.

My cock loves this, but it's not as sensitive since I just came. I can make it last now. I'm in great shape. My muscles are strong. I can fuck him like this for probably an hour if he wants.

He wants.

We fuck in all sorts of positions with Armstrong on his back with his legs in the air, or on his side, or standing at the foot of the bed bent over, but on his knees is best because I can mold him to my will. For just under one hour we fuck before we drop, exhausted, into mutual puddles of sweat. We had simultaneous orgasms. Mine ripped through me. So good. Now we are damp and covered in sweat, but who cares. He lies back on the bed and talk, not wanting to move, our muscles like liquid.

"Have you heard the latest rumor?" he asks, still gasping. His fire-dark eyes gleam.

With my cheek pressed against his warm, outstretched hand, I ask, "Which one?"

"Well, I heard from Hunter who heard it from Sigourney. They say someone on board is a scientist masquerading as a Hero. Supposedly Sig overheard it Earthside at the bon voyage festival. This plot's definitely not in the script. Or the job description."

"This is the first time I've heard it," I say. I sit up, still shaky, and scoot back to lean against the heated metal bulkhead where the bed lines up. From here, the view over my bunk and out the view screen is a treasure trove with my enhanced magnification screen. The texture of stars is silken; it makes the bulkheads glow.

Armstrong turns onto his stomach and rests his chin on a jeweled fist. (Rings are his favorite ornament.) His perfect backside shines in the sidereal light, copper-brown. "I've been trying to figure out who. And well, it has to be Danielle, don't you think?"

"Danielle?"

"She just isn't the Hero type, Stir. Haven't you noticed? She's strange. She's not playing to the cameras, she doesn't like multiple sex partners, she's stuck on her brother, and the most damning peculiarity of all, she's smart."

I shake my head. "She's no scientist. She's just disillusioned. With five missions back-to-back, she's tired. And she likes to act smart but it's all a performance. I can see right through her."

Armstrong shrugs. "I don't know. Who else could it be?"

"Well, Drac, maybe," I say. "Danielle is way protective of him."

"Nah." Armstrong disagrees. "He's too gorgeous, probably the best looking guy on board. No offense."

"None taken."

"And he's kinda dumb. I tried to start a conversation with him once and he looked flustered. He couldn't even use the food dispensers at first. I had to show him."

"Yeah, I had a similar experience. He's the strong and silent type, but kinda dumb, yeah. He was hired because of his looks obviously. It's his first voyage. He's just shy and Danielle is showing him the ropes. He'll come around."

"I suppose. Anyway, rumors are just rumors sometimes. Nothing to worry about," Armstrong says, though

13

the conviction is missing from his deep, usually booming voice.

"If it's true," I say, grasping the end of my bleach-blond ponytail and brushing it across my lips, "what would be the point of putting a scientist on *Lacrosse*?"

"To muck it up? Make us look bad?" Armstrong guesses.

I inhale. My hair smells like sex. I totally need a shower. "Why?"

He rolls to his side. There's a damp imprint of his body on the smooth sheet. The starlight tries to absorb it. "I've heard the technicians and scientists back home want back in space. Maybe if we fail, they can get public support?"

"Hmm." I watch the porthole, the silent, night-woven fields we Heroes love so much. Nothing moves. It's as if we're at a standstill and not hurtling six-hundred-twenty-eight million kilometers in eight weeks to the largest planet in our solar system.

I suddenly have the urge to write bad poetry. Armstrong, whose specialty is drama, will later recite it. Stuff like this is what the public craves. It's something our scientists seem incapable of giving. Our fans pay well for holos of our months in space. And we treat them to every delicacy, from sex to sculpture to daring acrobatic space-walks. Our lives are a performance. Art.

Armstrong suggests, "You should check into the background of everyone on board. As captain, you're the only one with access."

That would be real work, something I'm not used to. The script never calls for a real mystery where the loose ends aren't already figured out and programmed for us. This is supposed to be a straight-forward voyage, filled mainly with sex and traditional psychological tension. Armstrong and I even have a high-charged lover's quarrel prepared for the return trip.

But now everything is wrong. With Danielle breaking character and acting smart, even scientific-like, the camaraderie is off-balance. And now if the rumor is true, well, I don't want to think about the money I'm going to lose when those royalties don't come. Real life is a bore. No one will buy the recordings of this voyage if we have a real problem to solve.

"Moon crap," I sigh.

Chapter Three

I delay researching the rumor.

There are two reasons for my procrastination.

One: After my hot session with Armstrong, my ratings went up. That's more money for me. Bottom line: Sales are good. Why fuck with the program if it's going well?

Two: I'm not sure I need to know the truth. Or want to know. If I act innocent, even ignorant of what might be going on, none of this falls on me, right?

Except technically I am the captain. It is my role. And if my behavior deviates from that role, will my acting be called into question?

We are method actors. We are highly rated because we are good. If our behavior becomes contrived, self-conscious or false, the viewers notice and leave bad reviews. Bad reviews, if you get enough of them, can end a career.

We are actors, yes, but we must be natural, be ourselves. You can't pretend to like sex in space. The pleasure has to be somewhat real for you, or you're fucked.

I find myself conflicted.

The only other time this happened was when I thought I might actually be falling in love. That was a long time ago, my second mission. I was newer. Younger. A part of my brain could not help but equate really great sex and all those endorphins with falling in love.

I'd been extra crew back then on another ship. A low-ranked grunt. John Luke had been my captain. He was older, experienced, and made my mind fly. I had orgasms with him that lasted whole minutes. I craved him. I wanted to stay up nights just fucking him all night long.

The script called for a love affair without saying who, when or for how long. He took me into that script. He seduced me well, even wined and dined me.

I spent that voyage in a state of euphoria, and it nearly killed me to find out he did not feel the same. He enjoyed me, of course, but he was a pro and he knew how to keep himself aloof. John Luke did not form attachments. At least not for long.

He let me down gently. Over time.

The fans ate it up.

I even cried. To this day, only John Luke knows my tears weren't glycerin, but real.

It took me a few weeks after that voyage to settle. The rush of chemistry I'd felt between us—me and John Luke—subsided. I called myself all kinds of fool and moved on.

I've told no one this, but I still feel twinges to this day when I think of him, when I roll my eyes at my young self for being so naïve, so easily confused. Maybe what I felt was real, but John Luke did not return the real feelings, and so nothing could ever have come of it.

I protect myself well, now. I've learned how to have fun and be careful with my emotions. I learned how to leave all my tenderness at the door, and focus on the physical pleasures. The good times. Even friendship is allowed with me, but only so far.

This is how I prefer it.

I am never lonely.

Or so I tell myself. At any rate, I never lack for attention. That's for sure.

*

I distract myself with other crew. Beautiful bodies. Sweat gleaming in view screen starlight. Hunter with her gold-mesh fashion sense. Shariff with his Caribbean blue eyes. And as much of Armstrong as I can get. He's so fun and open.

I'm careful to watch my crew for real attachments, but they're all professional. Tried and true. Even Danielle, who's been such a cock-tease, lightens up over the next week or so.

She goes for the female crew, mostly, and I see it gets her ranking points. She won't let me at her, but that's all right. The tension that may or may not exist between us plays well for the script.

On my part, though I find her yearningly beautiful, it's her brother's mystique that plays with my brain. I can't get the rumor out of my head.

Is he undercover? What's his agenda? Will he hurt this mission and all our royalties?

Every time I try to get close to him, he finds an excuse to be elsewhere. That is, if he even ventures out of his nest.

For example, today he comes out for a quick meal. I happen to be in the mess hall when he arrives, literally on the coattails of Danielle. By literally, I mean she is wearing a long, diaphanous wrap about a tight purple skinsuit, and it trails in her wake. He walks so close to her the ends of the wrap flutter and caress his shins and thighs.

His head is up, though, not down like sometimes, and his black hair shines like space itself. It curves about his beautiful face, shadowing and highlighting the light bronze contours of his cheeks.

He's dressed all in black, as usual. This time his pants are low cut with disturbingly enticing "V's" below his navel and at the back, exposing half his ass.

He's tight everywhere. A vision. Skin, muscle, sinew all long-limbed and flexing. His arms are bare, his tank top black net leaving nothing to the imagination. One beige nipple pokes through a hole in the net, hard.

We're used to beautiful bodies in our line of work. If we don't come by them naturally, we buy them. Of course Drac must be enhanced. So it shouldn't matter to me. Just another beautiful guy on my crew. I'll fuck him good and when we return home, the vids will sell like hotcakes.

So why do I stare more intently? Why does my entire being gravitate toward him? Is it simply the mystery? The rumor?

But it feels like hot tendrils on the air putting out feelers, probing me, just to be near him. My body heats and chills. Spikes of pleasure zing through my arms, legs, belly, and groin. I'm instantly hard when he's near.

Do the others feel it, too?

I glance around me. Hunter is eating and looking at a vid on her tablet. She doesn't even look up. Armstrong is making coffee. He does look up, but then he looks at me, one eyebrow raised, and gives me a half-shrug. He's suspicious, but not hard.

Just another pretty face. Coming for breakfast.

Drac glances once at me, then away. He moves around his sister and takes a seat without getting himself any food or drink. He has a tablet in his hand and sets it on the table, immediately turning it on.

I'm at the end of the table, finishing my scrambled eggs.

Danielle goes to Armstrong. They talk low, then she takes two cups of coffee back to the table. She sets them down, one right in front of Drac, and looks up at me.

"Morning, Captain."

I nod. "Danielle." I look at Drac, whose head is bowed now, hair half-covering his face. "Morning, Drac."

Drac tilts his head without looking away from his tablet. "Um hum."

The script does have general descriptions within it. Drac is arrogant, standoffish. Plus, this is his first mission. He doesn't have much rank. He is supposedly learning the ropes. His sister is like his mentor. If there is more between them, I haven't seen the recordings yet.

But there must be some already on the market, I'm thinking, because he already ranks high and taboo sex, last year's trend on Earth, might maintain a lot of followers. Still, he's brand new. So why would someone who is unknown and stays to themselves (or with only his sister) be so quickly alluring? Even the best don't chart the numbers so quickly.

And yet he is alluring. Even to me, a seasoned pro.

"What are you learning about today, Drac?" There must be *some* conversation. The scene cries for it.

"Hyper-drives." His answer comes out in a monotone.

"Good."

"He learns fast," Danielle puts in.

"Hope it's not all work and no play." I smile. I'm a friendly captain. The kind who loves his crew. In more ways than one.

"Drac is still getting used to space," Danielle puts in.

"Of course." I nod.

"He's not spacesick, is he?" Hunter asks from her place down the long table.

"No," Danielle says.

"Can't he answer for himself?" she asks.

Drac sighs, tapping his screen, then glances up but does not look at any one of us. Instead, his eyes roam the ceiling. "I am not spacesick," he assures us in a firm tone.

"Well, if you have any problems, we all have pointers. There's sickbay if things get dicey."

"No problems. No spacesickness," he replies. He blinks, looks to the side and briefly meets my eyes. His are dark and bright. Something alive is behind them. Something excited, nervous, but also kept hidden. I see it briefly. I could flatter myself and think it's me that he finds me attractive. But I know it's something else. More. He says, "If I feel any symptoms, I'll inform you and sickbay at once."

"Good." I keep my voice neutral but my heart is fluttering at that look in his eyes, something grand, exciting. Shining. Like he's about to pop. This is what the vids are showing the fans back home on Earth. It's subtle, but you can't miss it. They are eating it up. But what is it?

The mystery keeps them watching.

It keeps me wanting.

I'm the captain, so I can give orders. Quickly, I come up with one. "I'd like updates on your progress. Meet me in my office this afternoon at two?"

The corner of Drac's mouth turns up. This is the most response I've seen to any of my inquiries or attempts to start conversations with him since the mission began.

"You want to talk about hyper-drives?" he asks.

"Anything you're learning. I live for progress reports." I give him my perfect smile and my best flirtatious posturing without looking too overt.

"I'm sure you do," he says.

It's almost as if he's patronizing me. Almost. But not quite. Because his look isn't disgusted, or hostile, or anything like that. It's more indulgent. As if I am a child.

Even that feeling turns me on. It's not weird. I like bossy lovers. It would be more than okay if Drac bossed me around. Naked. In bed.

"See you then." I get up, quickly take my plate to the disposal unit, and turn to grab my coffee.

I look toward Drac, but he's back to his tablet again, tapping and reading, his hair glowing, his posture perfect, the "V" in the back of his pants showing the upper half of his ass-crack. Taut cheeks on either side. Two dimples accenting the smooth knobs of his lower spine. The shadow in the crack is like a beacon. My cock twitches as if to say, "Home."

I'm stupidly infatuated. And he couldn't care less.

I think of John Luke. I'm not going to repeat that mistake again, that's for sure.

Chapter Four

Why am I nervous?

I sit at my clear, plasti-glass desk in my office playing with my lucky coin, an old Earth relic. A gold dollar with the image of Sacagawea on it. I flip it over my fingers back and forth, a magician's trick I used to practice for hours when I was a plain and lonely kid.

The viewport to my left shows dark space but I've used the screen controls to enhance the image to purples, blues and greens. They whirl at random, as if we are on the outskirts of a quasar.

Everything in my office is shiny and clean and reflects that light in soft glows: on my desk, against the bulkheads, puddling on the smooth flooring where my plush, black rug ends. I can't see myself, but I imagine my blond hair is tinted by that light as well, flirts of peacock tint.

I know I look good. But will Drac think so?

Just asking myself that question makes me even more nervous. I don't get insecure about my looks. Ever. I'm made for this job. I love it.

The coin flips faster across my knuckles, then falls to the floor with a sharp clang and jingles to a rest. I'm staring at it as the buzzer on my door goes off.

"Enter."

Drac walks in, so lean and tall he could look awkward, but he isn't. He's perfect. He moves like he's had ballet lessons, shoulders back, arms at his sides, feet firm on the deck.

My breath catches in my throat. I swallow hard. He's a dark-edged beauty and he intimidates me like no one ever has.

I'm immune to shyness or nerves. Over the years I've developed into a goddamn preening narcissist and not ashamed of it. I'm always in a role, and it's easy. Life is a charm for me. But Drac knocks me right off my pedestal and my mind becomes filled with voices, all my own but saying different things.

You want him so bad, but what if he's an ass?

Rumors say he has eyes only for his sister.

This is his first flight and rumors of a scientist aboard lean toward him.

He's dangerous which will make this fun.

He's dangerous which will make this forced, contrived.

The viewers will love you.

The viewers will hate you because you'll fuck up and come too fast. Or you will, for the first time in your life, not be able to get it up.

I had performance anxiety only twice in my life. My first time right after the makeover had me still getting used to this body belonging to me. I fucked a gorgeous crewman on the way to the Moon. I let him have me again and again, in all ways, flushed and open, but I was shaking the whole time and could not maintain an erection.

I hid it well from the cameras. But Tobi knew and treated me gently when I needed it, soft and slow and sweet. I climbed the charts fast. If the camera adds ten pounds, well, it also shows every vulnerability. If you're skittish and your eyes flick about, it can show that ten times more than you might be feeling it. My vulnerability, lucky for me, ended up playing great to the audience and I rose fast in the charts and in my roles on future voyages into space.

The second time I had performance anxiety was when I realized I was in love with John Luke but it was unrequited. I was required to continue to fuck him at least two more times on the way back to Earth after our mission was completed.

I said I cried. Well, only in private. I did not show my tears to my fans. But my body closed itself off from him. It took all his sexual talents—and he had many—to get me off. Our ratings tanked and I left John Luke with a confused smirk on his face. There had been anger in his steel blue eyes.

Afterward, I went to my agent and said I needed it to be in all my future contracts that I would never work with John Luke again. When my agent asked me why, I refused to answer. But he obeyed.

Now Drac stands before me, and those sorts of feelings rise up in me. An anxiety I haven't felt in years. But I'm the captain, and this is my mission. I tell myself there is no way some upstart, no matter how magnificent, is going to get the best of me.

Oh, but he's wearing those same trousers, the ones with the "V" in the front that shows his shaved abdomen almost to the base of his cock. You can see the way the skin begins to dent there, and the curve of his junk begins just at the leather's edge. His skin is tan, firm. The abdomen taut with flat, hard muscle.

He changed out of his tank from this morning. Now he wears a leather vest treated with something that looks like dye or paint. Orange, gold and red, diffused. His shoulders are bare, broad and striped with sinew just beneath the flesh. His chest is bare as well, gleaming. All the men present six-packs, but his are less defined. There, but not overt. Lean and smooth.

I think touching him would be like touching brushed silk over steel.

Drac seems to sense I am speechless in this moment. My eyes roving over him make no secret of my admiration. He twitches his shoulders once, and takes the lead I had meant to take in this scene.

"What is this meeting about?" Drac asks.

"You know what it is about," I say. "I want updates. Mission reports on how you are fitting in. This is your first mission. I want to see you do well. And I want you to know I'm here if you have any questions."

He does not smile in welcome to my words as any usual green recruit would do. Most would be hoping like hell for a seduction about now.

Drac remains stoic, almost accusatory as he says, "I don't have questions. And I'm doing fine."

"You stay to yourself. You're not on duty as much as I'd like to see."

"A lot of my job can be done from my computer in my quarters."

"I see."

He stares at me, brown gaze clear, almost challenging. He's young and healthy. He's smart. But smart enough to be a scientist? Even if the rumors are going around, I can't believe it. And yet, his behavior…

"Well," I continue. "I like to see my crew mingle. I need to see them at their stations or on breaks together, at least a few hours a day. It's not healthy to stay cooped up for too long. Cabin fever is real out here in the pitch. We're nowhere and have only each other. It's imperative for mental health to interact."

He smiles, and it is part acting, part knowing. Like he's in on a secret, but not with me. I hate it. I love it. I want to bend him over and show him who's boss.

He's standing there like caged steel. Dark and foreboding. Yet at the same time young, innocent.

"Please sit. If you don't have questions, I do," I say.

He eyes the soft black chair attached to the deck in front of my desk. Then looks toward the pale blue couch against the left bulkhead.

"You aren't in a hurry, are you?"

He knows the answer. I haven't given him any other orders than this meeting. He has nothing else to do. But he hesitates.

"Go on," I encourage. I am feeling stronger now. My voice less breathy.

I want him. Yes. But I also want to know him. That's not always the case. For example, Armstrong and I talk, but not about anything personal. I don't really know him except he's a great actor and fantastic in bed.

But Drac is different. I want to know where he comes from. I want to know why he decided to sign on. Why he's here when he stays away from people. This is a movie. An adult movie in many of its scenes. And he has not played up to that. It's damned unusual. But I am not going to say that to him.

Drac sits in the black chair, leaning with his arms resting on the armrests and his legs stretched, ankles crossed. It is as if he has made that chair his throne. He owns it. Like he does this scene.

I can imagine the audience grinning. Upping Drac's rank.

"I am quite up to date in all my duties," Drac begins.

But not up to date on the mingling. Not the drama, and definitely not any sort of sex that I am aware of, soap opera or other. The rumors of him and Danielle are suggestive only. I've looked at the tapes.

"All of them?"

The edge of his mouth quirks up. "And what duty have I not yet accomplished, Captain?"

The statement should sound filthy. But in his voice and tone, again, it is almost accusatory.

The script calls for sex in my office during meetings. All the time. There can be exceptions which I can manipulate as the captain, but Drac doesn't know that.

"I have to wonder."

"What is that?" he asks.

"If you like anything you see aboard this ship."

He shrugs but his eyes dart away. Only for a second, but the cameras will catch it. They miss nothing. And that gesture will be multiplied by big screens and fancy lighting back home.

"I like plenty that I see," Drac says, gaze full on me now.

I nod. I don't want to be cheesy or overt. I want this to look natural. But it's damn hard because Drac is not forthcoming. He's an ass. It makes me want him even more.

He's a challenge and it seems real. I like it.

My pulse revs up. My cock twitches. He is just my type. Strong. Exuding power even though he's a newbie and probably far younger than I.

John Luke gave off this sort of vibe. But he was the captain. Now I am the captain. It should be all turned around. It has been for years. I have my crew flock to me. Want me. Need me.

But I want Drac. It feels as if he's in charge. I need him. I hadn't realized, until meeting him, being on board ship with him this past week, how much I missed this dynamic. I'd closed myself off to it after John Luke. It has been forever. But now my skin tingles. My blood heats.

"Where are you from, Drac?"

"You already know. My file—"

"I like to hear it face to face," I interrupt. In truth, I only scan the files. I like to get to know my crew and my lovers through live, hands on experience. A digital checklist speaks facts but not necessarily truth. By that I mean personality, heart, and mind. How a person laughs or smiles, kisses or comes in your arms cannot be reduced to an organized processing of words and symbols through a computer program.

Maybe Drac's favorite color is yellow, but what shade of yellow? Light gold like the stars through a shaded visor? Or dark yellow like daffodils in spring? He may have muscles measured to the inch in his bio, but it says nothing of their tone, how hard they may feel, how soft the skin. Or how that skin might blush darker, pinker under the right touch, the cleverest of stimulation. The files never state how a person can smell of fresh rain, or cut grass, or if their semen tastes like the sea. It says nothing about how they kiss, if it's sloppy and slobbery, or cool and clean and deep.

Drac is succinct. "I grew up in San Diego. But I was born in Greece."

This explains his Greek god looks. Well, that and perhaps a bit of surgical intervention.

"Were you and your sister close?"

He tilts his head. A sign of secrets, or is he affronted? I can't tell.

"Danielle is ten years older and helped raise me."

"Ah, the big sister."

"Yes."

"Sounds nice. She probably protected you. If anyone was mean to you, she'd take them down."

"Are not all older siblings protective of the younger ones?" he asks.

"I would like to hope so."

"Did she help you get this job?"

"In a manner of speaking. But I got it on my own merits as well."

More hints he is not who he appears. Or is that my overactive imagination combined with the rumor mill?

"What merits?"

"It's all in your file."

"I like to hear what you think."

His beautiful chest heaves. He takes a deep breath. "I passed all the tests. Physical. Psych. Even I.Q. Not too smart, not too dumb."

And just the right amount of pretty. But he doesn't need to say it since the surgeons can fix anything in that area that fails to pass muster in a matter of days.

"Social?"

"Are you questioning my stats on that test?"

Honestly, I haven't looked. I should have. But I scanned all the files before boarding, before I knew what a hermit he was.

Now I wonder. He makes even this conversation difficult. It's not the way of our missions, or in any of the scripts I've ever seen. By now we should be kissing, groping. Hungry-eyed for each other.

And I am hungry. But it feels more desperate than usual, like if I mess this up I'll be crying. I'll be out. John Luke did a number on me, but I thought I was over it. It's been so many years.

"Hobbies?" I ask to keep the chat going.

"Like you with your poetry?"

I nod. My eyes flick to the gold coin on the floor. "And sometimes magic."

At that, his eyebrows go up. "There's no such thing as magic."

I laugh. It feels good, loosens me up a little. "No such thing as magicians? Magic tricks?"

"Oh, I thought you meant…" He trails off, his lips pressing tight.

New. Young. Naïve.

I get up from my chair and bend over to pick up the coin. I go to the front of my desk and lean against it, closer to him. He has a noir scent, spice and vanilla. My blood surges. I want to taste him.

Instead, I take the coin and dribble it over the tops of my fingers. Faster and faster.

He says, "Do you juggle, too?"

I laugh again. "Apples. Oranges. Knives." I pause. "Balls. People."

He laughs now. I ease closer to him. I flip the coin toward him. He reaches up to catch it, misses. It clatters and jingles to the bare deck and lands silent and soft on the black rug that runs along the viewport.

His gaze follows the coin. He does not move.

I watch him carefully. "I can teach you."

He glances at me, then back to the coin. His thick, dark lashes make shadows on his cheeks.

He swallows. "I might—uh—like that." His voice has softened. It creates a tremble inside me.

I move to grab the coin up, then approach him. All business of course. I show him slowly how I balance the coin, how I flip it using the spaces of my fingers, how the muscles know how to grab and pull and push all at once with years of practice.

"You won't get it right first try." I place the coin in his hand.

"I know." He is looking down. He moves the coin where I tell him. He follows my instructions. It falls several times. I touch his hand. He lets me manipulate his fingers. He is warm and vibrant and alive. He gives off an energy my body can't help but crave.

After about a dozen tries, he manages to flip it once.

"Practice," I say. "You can keep that."

It's my lucky coin. I am never without it. My impulse to give it to him is odd. But not. If it really is lucky, the object of my affections should have it.

Drac looks up at me. "This is old. An antique."

I nod. "It's okay. I just hope you don't sell it."

He shakes his head.

I want to touch his hair. So badly. Or his cheek.

For what seems like a long minute but is probably only seconds, we are close, our breaths synchronized. Poems of longing demand to be written. But later.

Damn me for not scrutinizing his file harder. But what would it tell me? I already know. This is his first mission.

And then I realize he's never filmed before. Or maybe he has, but not the types of vids we're doing. I don't remember his file showing a list of his roles in other vids. Or holos. He's not a seasoned actor.

A virgin?

Certainly not sexually, but as a performer. As a space dude on a ship of porn stars. And I remember again my first times with Tobi and that nervous trip to the Moon.

Softly, "Have dinner with me."

Wait. We don't normally date out here in the stars.

Well, I'm doing it now.

Drac says, "Why?"

I frown. "I like talking to you. Bring the coin. Practice. Show me if you can get two flips without dropping it."

"Dinner is two hours from now."

"Then you better practice hard. I want to see improvement." But I'm joking. Grinning. I start to reach out to give him a little shoulder push. I hesitate and don't touch.

Drac slides out of the chair, his leather slipping against the plush material, and avoids my gesture. He gives me a nod without meeting my eyes.

He heads for the door and I admire his backside, the dimples, the upper part of his crack revealed by the back "V" of the trousers.

Gods. My cock actually hardens.

The door opens and he exits into the corridor, his fist bunched tight around the gold coin.

It's a start.

Chapter Five

After Drac leaves, I speak to my computer. "Bring up Drac's files."

"Done." It speaks in a sweet female voice.

Still standing by the front of my desk, I turn to look out the viewport. Sapphire. Amethyst. Swirls of space. I do not go back to my desk. I do not look at Drac's files. They won't help me get to know him.

Of course I could dig deeper than those files. I could initiate Earth background checks. I could network with PTB computer systems.

But I don't. I won't. I want to know him as he is now. Maybe it's a role he's playing, but I still want it. Him.

I leave my office and go to the bridge.

I sit for a while with my tablet. Stray words come, but nothing solid. Nothing more than fragments of sentences.

My poetry is published, but I'm not great. People like it because I wrote it in space. Because I'm already a celebrity as Captain Stirling Kane of the *Lacrosse*.

I tap on the screen: *Space, like an infinite dark wine... a glass of shadows... salted with stars...*

Nothing to send home to my editor. Nothing about Drac because words fail me. Longing poems are cliché. Love poems worse, although my agent says they would sell even better than my space poems. But somehow they're too personal. I fill notebooks with them just for me. About the very thing I'm missing. Tension. Cravings. Obsession. Wanting to know someone so well it is like a merging where you finish each other's sentences, where you can't always tell where one leaves off and the other begins. Shiny dark hair. Messy blond. Interweaving.

Yes, sometimes I do write poems like that and keep them to myself.

I toss my tablet aside, tempted to delete everything I've just put down.

The usual shallow thoughts return. Not a captain's thoughts. Just the old me. Weldon Philbert from long ago so thrilled to be included with the cool crowd, an actor shooting through the void.

I wonder what I should wear to dinner. This is my first date in years.

*

The mess hall is busy. There is no privacy. I do my best to ignore the comings and goings of my crew, their loud, half-drunken conversations, and set up plates and wine glasses. I find a nice white wine in the galley stores. I'm heating up pre-made fettuccini with Alfredo sauce.

Armstrong and Hunter come into the galley section and comment on my set up. Smirk and laugh a little.

"Jealousy does not become you," I say.

They link arms and leave together for more comfortable settings to do dirty deeds.

I sit and wait. And wait.

Drac does not show.

I wait half an hour before heading for his quarters and buzzing to be let in.

No answer.

I hit the bypass. I am the captain. I can do that. What if it's an emergency?

The door opens. I see Drac at his desk hunched forward, fingers flying over his keyboard. Voice low and rumbling some command.

He jerks as the door opens, glancing up. "Captain—"

"I've been waiting." I make a pose at the threshold of the door. It should frame me nicely for the holo-vids.

I had decided to wear my black coat lined in purple satin. It even has tails. I wear no shirt underneath, and tight black pants. It's becoming. But while I do things like pose in

33

fancy garments without effort, on auto-pilot so to speak, I'm not exactly playing around here. I'll admit to some emotion in play.

Drac frowns. "The time is only —" He looks at his screen, then up again. "I didn't notice. I didn't forget."

"I am never stood up."

He gets to his feet. "No. I'm sure you never are." He has not changed for our date, but that's okay. I'm becoming obsessed with those leather trousers. And that multi-sunset-hued vest.

Drac pushes his hand through his perfect hair, tangling it, making part of it stick out at the side. It's endearing. And frustrating.

"I am hungry," he says.

Well, I never expected him to be a romantic.

"Good. I've got food heating. And wine." I turn and start to walk down the corridor. I hear him following me, his footfalls rapid and light since he is barefoot.

We enter the mess. It's empty, thank the gods. I had lit a cheap candle and it's guttering, having burnt itself to a white, waxy nubbin.

"Smells good," he says.

I can't really smell the dinner, but I can smell the burning candle which overpowers the room. I want to turn to him and give him a light slug. It's not violence he's driven me to. I just want to get him to wake up a little.

"Yeah, burnt candle for dinner," I reply.

"Oh." He sits. Of course he takes the chair I had intended for myself.

I lean over him and pour our wine. The goblets reflect the bulkhead lighting, low-energy blue and white mixing with the gold of the wine itself splashing up the sides of the glass.

I go to the galley which is an open room right off the mess hall, and serve up two plates of fettuccini. It does look and smell good.

I bring the food to the table with a small basket of warm garlic bread.

Garlic is not supposed to be a date thing, but I like it. I don't care. And I know Drac has no clue about the etiquette of wining and dining someone.

Drac is at the head of the long table. I sit to his left.

"Parmesan?" I ask.

"No, thank you."

I don't take it, either. The sauce is rich enough. I mean, I work out. I don't have to watch my weight anymore since I changed from Weldon to Stirling. But my stomach is older now. I don't like the heaviness of too much rich food in large portions.

Drac takes a bite. "Very good," he comments.

"I'm glad you like it."

We are silently eating for a good solid two minutes.

Finally, I can't take it any longer. "What were you working on so diligently that you forgot the time? A novel or something?"

"No. No, nothing like that. Just some of my hobbies."

"Tell me."

"They wouldn't interest anyone."

"Try me."

"It's like a game with numbers," he says.

"A holo?"

He shakes his head. "More like a puzzle. Numbers, no people."

"Oh. Like Sudoku or something?"

"Or something." His head bows. He shovels in more pasta. He's a good eater, so there's that. Along with the handsome stuff going on. He even chews in a sexy way, his jaw tightening, strong and firm with every crunch.

His dark eyes lighten when he tries the garlic bread.

"Fantastic," he says, mouth full.

I smile. "Good to know." Garlic was never going to be a problem between us. That's one win.

"So what do you think of your first time in space?"

His eyes sparkle. "It's amazing! I am thrilled by it. How everything on this ship works, the scents, the sounds… I'm in awe."

That was the most excitement I'd ever seen from him. And it wasn't about fucking; it was about the ship.

I can actually relate to him on that level. I love the ship myself. "I can stand by a viewport for an hour and look out and not notice the time passing."

Drac's smile is the most beautiful smile I've ever seen. He stops eating. He looks at me like he is hungry. Hungry for more of this. My words. It is a start.

"I have a live feed of three of the ship's ports up on my computer at all times."

"Really? At first it made me dizzy whenever I walked by a viewport," I say.

"Me, too!" His chest rises and falls.

"Years ago. I got used to it in a few days."

"I'm still getting used to it."

I have the stupid shallow thought I wish it is me who makes him dizzy. Well, we have time.

"You write about space a lot."

Surprised, I nod. He has not offered a comment on me or my habits until now. Frankly, I had the notion he forgot I existed this afternoon. He hadn't really stood me up, he'd just forgotten the time, so he said.

I pick up my wine glass and take some sips. It's earthy and good.

"I've read some of your work."

I almost spit out that last sip. I lean forward and set my glass down. "What?"

"I sampled *The Texture of Stars*."

"Oh?" My *most* famous book. Just a lot of rambling, though.

"You're very good."

I blink. "Oh?"

I recall a lot of critical derision and fun at my expense. *The Porn Star Poet*, some have called me. *Talent has nothing to do with this book's popularity. Anyone can get a hit book if they are already a celebrity,* is the one review I remember. It isn't false, but my heart beat more painfully in my chest a few days after that one. I remember smatterings of others: *Silly descriptions that make no sense. These poems have no depth or story. Amateur at best.* I get good reviews sometimes, too, but one tends to remember the bad, right?

I stopped reading any of my reviews years ago on my books and my vids. But my publisher sells those books, and insists I turn over whatever new pages I come up with. It's only the love poems I keep close to my heart. Secret.

"I'm just a dabbler."

Drac's eyebrows rise. "I think not. You have seven bestselling books to your credit. For poetry. That's a difficult feat in itself. People don't read poetry."

"But you do?"

"I glanced at yours before boarding."

"Why?"

"I wanted to know who was running this ship."

"Surely you've seen the recordings."

"No." He looks away. "I haven't."

"But what made you want to become an actor? Sign on for this job?"

His eyelids half-close. "I wanted to experience going into space. All of this."

He glances about the mess as if it's the most beautiful place he's ever been with its white cabinets, white bulkheads, long square tables and simple black chairs fastened to the deck. This room has one piece of art on the wall, a sort of faux stained glass of red, yellow and brown leaves. The huge port is on the far wall taking up most of the space, and is turned to normal view, showing only blackness out there, thick and empty.

I grab my wine again, take more than a sip. It's weird he doesn't comment on the vids or watch them. The soap opera we are part of. It's the number one thing about these missions. The rest is for some boring, scientific survey group back on Earth to go over, to control, and that's all on auto.

But Drac is interested in that? Not the sex?

Armstrong is right. We do have a scientist on board. Well, hobbyist at the very least.

Drac has motives other than acting and I've never met anyone like him.

But I do not accuse him of being a scientist, amateur or otherwise. It's a bad word out here, and I'm not into name-calling. Also, it could ruin his career here, if he wants to keep at the acting/filming part, I mean.

"That's interesting."

He sighs. "Not very."

"Is that why you have been more shy? Your first time out here and you're more thrilled about space bodies than the pretty ones on board?"

He's silent.

"It's normal to be nervous," I assure him.

"Danielle says the same."

"She's right."

"Well, it's not a crime. Your hobbies can be anything you want. But you realize they affect your ratings. Not that you have anything to worry about that yet. You're pretty high already."

"I am?"

"You haven't checked?"

He shakes his head.

"You're doing well."

"I don't see why. I haven't done anything yet."

"Have you looked in the mirror?" I ask.

He starts to roll his eyes and stares down at his food.

"People like a handsome mystery."

"I suppose they do." His voice is low, almost defeated.

"I know I do."

He starts to glance up, then stops. "I'm just on some checklist. But all right. Will the hook up be in your quarters, then?"

I'm stunned at his words. "A checklist?"

"Yes. That's how this works, right?"

He is right. That is how this works. So how can I tell him this date, this dinner and our conversation has made me interested in *him*? That doesn't happen to me. Would he even believe me?

"You'll go through the entire crew on this voyage at least ten times each, right?" he asks.

"I thought you didn't watch my vids." But my inner thoughts sound defensive. *You said you never watch my vids. You don't know anything about me.*

"I understand the formula."

How he talks. Like a real scientist. "This is an equation to you?" But somehow, him being different, it's hot. It has me intrigued and defensive and ready to defend my honor all at once.

"Everything is."

"Even sex?"

"Of course. Body chemistry. Hormones. Capillaries expand and contract. Pleasure is manifested."

"Manifested," I echo. "Interesting choice of word to describe an erotic condition. Or love."

"Love?" he asks.

Nice segue into my own thoughts of late. I can't stop myself from asking, "Have you ever been in love?"

He looks at me with those intense eyes, still and calm. Finally, "No."

I clamp down hard on memories of John Luke. He was hard like that, too. Told me he'd never been in love and never intended to be. Like maybe it's my weakness to fall for that sort? A default of my own where I fall down a well of desire and longing to take that hard look and watch it melt under my talented hands, mouth and body?

Yes, I have a type. And I am doomed because of it. To feel more for those guys. Women, too, but I've yet to meet one with that particular look. And I prefer the men. Luckily, ninety-nine percent of the people I meet do not have that look.

So I've been safe from love. Safe and free and open to all opportunities.

"Have you?" Drac asks.

"What?" I had been distracted by my own thoughts.

"Been in love?"

I shrug and nod. "Once."

"I see." Maybe it's my imagination, but I think his eyes soften.

When I don't elaborate, he leans back. His plate of pasta is only half-finished, but he seems sated. He has not touched his wine. The candle has long since burned out from the guttering mess it was when we walked in.

"So you never answered my other question," Drac says.

"The one about the checklist."

"Yes."

"I don't want you to think like that. That you are some name on a list only. You're human. I'm human. It's a friendly ship. There's a script. But you are by no means required to do anything you don't consent to."

"I came aboard. Isn't that consent?" he asks.

"You know what I mean. You don't have to have a checklist. You don't have to go off with anyone you don't wish to, um, *be* with. That includes me."

He glances at me. Up and down as if seeing me for the first time. "I accepted your date."

A thrill courses through me. "Yes. You did. But I'm beginning to question your reasons." This is getting uncomfortable. I don't like being unwanted. If he has better places to be, I want to be let down now, not later.

"I accepted your date," he repeats.

"I heard you the first time."

"That means I said yes. I consent." He isn't looking at me, but again at the boring white walls. His lips do not curve up, but I sense a smile in the muscles of his face. His cheeks dip in. His chin firm.

"Well, that just enlivened the mood in here."

"What?"

"All this talk of chemicals in the body and checklists and consent." I squint at him. "So passionate."

He clears his throat. "I'm—I'm not used to this. I apologize."

Then why sign on for the job? I really should have opened the guy's file when I pulled it up. Done some sleuthing.

"You want to be here, don't you?" I lean my elbows on the table.

"I do." His hair brushes his shoulder like a graceful shadow.

"Well, it's your first voyage. There's always a transition phase. Longer for some than others."

"I'm mucking it up."

"No. You're being honest. Which I appreciate. I don't always get honesty. Actors, you know." I force a grin.

"Everybody's acting all the time to get what they want, aren't they? Here, back on Earth. In life."

"I suppose if you put it that way—"

"But you're frustrated. You expected more—passion." He looks up, muscles tight about the brow and his upper cheeks.

"I don't know what I expected."

I do some quick analysis of my own behavior. I've been shallow. I've been forward. I've been enamored, turned on because he's my type, but now I'm forced to look at what I might really want. Is Drac only a hook up to me? Am I fooling myself that I want him only in a physical way? Because I usually don't date. I don't wine and dine. I'm a total fiend. I have a boner for everyone. And I like to preen about the fact that they all want me back.

"Well, think about it. I'm asking you now," Drac says.

I lick my lips. My hands are folded tight in my lap. I don't have a boner right now. Which is warpy. Weird. "I like talking to you."

"Why?"

I laugh. "You ask hard questions. And that's one of them. I like it. It gets a lot the same up here, blank and boring."

"Pretty people, actors, scripts, poetry, ratings. Not *that* boring, I think. Exciting."

"Are you excited by that? You told me you haven't even checked your rating."

"I would be stupid if I said I wasn't flattered." He half-smiles and there's a curve of a dimple in his cheek.

"Yeah. It's a head-trip, all right. You get famous and some can't handle it. But you'll do fine."

He nods. "Maybe. So… you like talking to me? Really?"

"I wouldn't have said if I didn't mean it."

"Well, would you like to talk some more, then?"

My grin widens. "You asking me for a second date?"

His face darkens. There is a blush washing over him. It's amazing. Becoming. I love it.

"I guess I am," he answers.

"I accept."

"Tomorrow night? My quarters?"

"I'll be there." But now I'm even more enamored. Intrigued. Taken. What the fuck am I going to do for twenty-four hours waiting to see him again? Waiting to — talk. Just talk.

I haven't done this sort of thing since I was a kid.

It feels good.

Chapter Six

I roam the white corridors pretending to do a job. To be the captain. Even though I am the captain of *Lacrosse*, a title I am damned proud of, it's a label only. A role. I'm not really in charge of anything. That all goes to the PTB back on Earth.

But I get the badge, so to speak. Or the braid. There are no uniforms here in space, but the icon on my name all over the nets — my brand — shows it all. Pretty. Golden. Ornate.

I am not nervous about my second date with Drac. But I am killing time because it's all I can think of. All I want. I wish I could go to him now, but even though he hasn't said it in words, his behavior has made it pretty clear that he wants this strictly timed appointment. He wants to set that structure. Maybe he likes rules. Even though he stood me up on our first date — well, almost stood me up — he wants a plan.

So, okay then. It's moony-petunias on a ship like this within a script that's more porn than reality, but I'm agreeable. We'll date.

I guess it feels like I'm a kid again. I have all this built-up anticipation. I didn't sleep soundly during ship's night. I tossed and turned a lot. I kept seeing Drac's half-smile, and the way his eyes would go from hard to soft. They way he questioned me. The oddness of it all. And of course I could not forget how he finally — finally! — gave me the once-over, gaze moving down my body, then up at the end of our dinner conversation.

I keep telling myself he likes me. So stupid. What's not to like? More assumptions on my part, shallow dude that I am. I'm cute. So what? It's obvious it takes more than cute to impress him. He came to life when he talked about my poetry. My moronic poetry! Really? But my heart rate ramps up just remembering the praise, like my poetry is more important than my looks. Hard to believe. I may have books published of that stuff, but I still compartmentalize that from my life as if it's not real. It's an indulgence. Like some people knit. It's no biggie. Not a serious thing, anyway, just some fun. But it is creating. It is about the heart, but still separate from what's real, you know?

And my hidden notebooks. Those are really separate, in the far corner of my world… fantasyland meanderings. Just me muttering in my sleep. They are mine, but they are hidden as if behind a final layer of clothing I'll never take off in front of the cameras.

I go to the ship's gym and work out for a while with Armstrong. No sex. He doesn't ask. Seems the rumor mill has replaced the "scientist on board" whisperings with "the captain's dating??!"

I laugh it off.

I take a long sonic bath. The crystal blue energy fizzes about me and I relax and nap.

I skip lunch, something I never do. I tell myself it's not nerves. No way. I'm simply not hungry.

I play a holo. Not a sexy one this time. Just one where I'm catching and freezing aliens for further study. They all have different ways of being elusive and it's a puzzle to figure out. The scarlet ones with three heads are the worst.

I think more about researching Drac's file. But I hate research. Reading, if it's fiction, okay. But not real work. And besides, it's like peeping. Creepy, especially since Drac is going to be right in front of me and I can, in theory, ask him anything I want to know.

Finally the time arrives when I can start our second date. I practically run to his door and buzz my arrival.

He opens it. He looks — a little frazzled maybe. His hair is tangled but still with that bright, dark shine. He's wearing a half top, netted, in dark purple. And those same "V" leather pants.

I totally did my hair and eyes. You know, that tint of makeup that highlights but doesn't look like make up? I picked my outfit carefully to show off my attributes, tight, torn old-Earth jeans, white shirt and tie, gold vest. I am showing less skin, but the shirt accents my broad shoulders and lean waist and hips. I tucked it in and left the tie casual and loose, the top shirt button undone. I will admit, my hair is perfect. I used *Gloss-and-Shine* on it. The kind that doesn't leave it hard, but still styles it. It's loose. My bangs are pushed back except for one artful curl. The *Gloss-and-Shine* sponsors will be happy.

Drac glances about, as if he has someone else in the room he's hiding, but he doesn't. It's nerves. I laugh it off.

"Is it time?" he asks.

"You don't keep track of time very well, do you?"

"I get — engrossed."

"Yeah," I say. "I see that."

He ushers me inside. His room smells of conditioned air and coffee. Not bad. My stomach growls from not eating lunch.

Drac gestures for me to sit on a black couch facing a long, glass coffee table. There are two plates stacked there, and a couple of pink plastic glasses.

He goes to his wall fridge and opens the door, taking out two small paper wrapped packages and a bottle of Coke.

"I've got frozen burritos and Coke," he says, turning, graceful, unassuming. "If that's not great, I can go to the galley and find something better."

My mouth waters. "Are you kidding? I love it. I haven't had a frozen burrito in so long. They're incredible. And Coke. It's so hard to find these days. The ship's stores don't have any in stock. Where'd you get that?"

"I order large bottles by the crate from Netbay. Same with the burritos. I brought them aboard in my own private belongings."

I grin at him. "Why didn't I ever think of Netbay? But that must be expensive."

He doesn't comment on the exact cost, or say anything about if it's a hardship or not. "It's worth it."

Maybe he's a secret zillionaire. I bask in the idea, but not more than I bask in the sight of him, unconsciously beautiful, and serving me what he thinks is garbage but is really an event. I fucking love burritos.

He heats them up in a microwave all unit. It takes about thirty seconds. Then he serves them steaming on the plates he's set out. He fills the little plastic glasses with ice and pours the Coke over all that good coldness. The carbonation hisses.

We use our hands to eat.

"Unfuckingbelievable," I say between bites.

He gifts me a short chuckle.

The Coke is like drinking ambrosia straight from Olympus. He's a Greek god for sure.

We eat and start out casually conversing. It's nice. Relaxing. My nerves have forgotten to be tense.

"I like your tie," he says.

It's a shiny blue tie that catches different light colors at different angles. "Thanks."

I talk about spending part of my day catching aliens for further study. He smirks. He tells me he's been playing with numbers again.

"Did you write today?" he asks.

I shake my head no. "Too distracted."

"By what?" As he finishes asking the question, he seems to figure it out. His eyes roll. His smirk turns to a half-smile, the one that sends tingles of heat throughout my body.

As we are finishing up, and I'm on my second glass of Coke on the rocks, he says, "Would you ever show me one of your poems that you've never shown to anyone else?"

"You mean like something new?"

He shrugs. He can't know I hide a bunch of them. No one knows.

My face heats at the question because it's so personal. How could he know? My poetry is silly. A time-waster even if it makes me money. It's just strings of words. My inner thoughts. And stupid, now-becoming-ordinary descriptions of space. Planets strung like necklaces. Moons that look like winterscapes.

"I'll think about it. Maybe I'll have to get to know you better."

He nods knowingly. "And that's how I feel about sex."

I figured this out yesterday. Or maybe even before. He hasn't been hiding out with Danielle. He's been staying to himself. "Then why did you want this job?"

"I told you. I love space. I wanted to go. I convinced myself I could deal with the rest."

"You could have told me."

"Told you what? When? When I first came on board that I'm only here to stare into space, and if I become a cock-tease in the process, well, I'm sorry?"

I stare at him. "Well." I pause. "Uh, yeah."

He sighs loudly as he gets up to clean the table. "I thought I could do this."

I want to placate him badly. He's gotten under my skin. "It's all right."

"How?"

"Well, you're with me. I'm the captain. I fix things, right? That's what a captain does."

He approaches the table and sits, facing me. "You're different."

"From what?"

"From when you were two weeks ago when I first boarded."

"You didn't know me then." I smile.

"I know. You flirted. You played hard. You've already logged a bunch of vids. It's why you're rich. You know how to play to the market."

"I do." I take a deep breath.

"But you're different with me. Is it because I'm more difficult? Are you still using tactics to get me to bed?"

"Tactics? Like a battle?"

"Isn't everything a battle?" he asks.

"I'll tell you this much," I confess. "I haven't done this much talking to one person — the same person — in a year. And you've had me on edge all day. If that's tactics, then I've got them down pat and consciously don't know I'm doing it."

He leans back and crosses his arms over his chest.

This continues for some time. Our volley, like throwing the ball back and forth between us. Catching it better and faster each time.

He has opinions on everything and I love to see him get animated about a topic. He likes mystery holos, like me. But he doesn't have a single care about sports. He thinks all the planets could eventually be colonized — well, their moons at least — through terraforming. He likes to think about the future. He's way too animated about anti-gravity and how ships like ours could do these journeys in a day not only to the planets in our Solar System, but far-flung worlds as well.

"Ah, a science fiction fan." But then I think, why hasn't he ever seen a *Lacrosse* holo-vid starring Stirling Kane?

"You could say that."

I don't want to focus on the fact that he hasn't watched me in my starring role and ruin the night, so I don't ask him what his favorite vids are. Instead, I change the subject.

"Got any games you might like for two?"

I expect him to suggest a whole list of holo titles. Instead, he goes to his closet and brings out boxes. Dominoes. Chess. Backgammon.

"Hmm. Really?"

But I like his eccentricity.

We play all of them long into the night and I find it loosens me up. And him. We're both laughing at our moves, our wins, our defeats.

At the end, I don't feel like a goof-off or a joker or a flirt. Just a guy having fun with another guy. Before I leave, I say, "Tomorrow night? Same time? My quarters?"

"Yes," he says, voice low, and bows his head. It's wonderful. That reaction. It curls my toes.

"Bring the Dominoes."

"I will."

We stand at his door staring at each other for a moment. I want to reach out. Nothing too overt, just a touch on the shoulder. Before I can, he reaches instead. His hand rests lightly on my left shoulder.

"Thank you," he says.

"This was fun." My eyes go to where he's touching me. My face heats.

He gives me a wry smile. "Sleep well."

"You, too."

There's a spring to my step as I head to my own bed. Alone.

Chapter Seven

He shows up on time. A surprise I do not expect.

I don't have Coke to offer him, but I remembered how he didn't touch the wine on our first date, so I have iced tea instead. And strawberry milkshakes for dessert.

I've spent the day thinking of him. All day, actually.

Armstrong came by once in the early afternoon and asked if I was feeling okay. "The crew thinks you're avoiding them."

I reassured him. The crew is large enough, diverse enough; they don't need me to entertain them. They don't need all my attention. If they're jealous of Drac, that's their deal. And it could play well in the script, anyway. Everyone loves a little drama. And besides, Drac and me? It's none of their business.

Now Drac is here and my world is complete again. After only a few hours away from him, I've missed him.

He has brought the Dominoes. We eat and play with them for a little while, and grow more and more at ease. I learn he was a nerd in school, head of the chess club. I wasn't head of anything like that, but also a nerd in school. An outcast. I feel free enough, finally, to tell him my name used to be Weldon, not Stirling.

When he doesn't laugh, when he only smiles and tilts his head like he's thinking it's not so bad, that I'm not a complete flibbertigibbet, that's the moment I know for sure. I'm in love with this hard-edged dude who lives on frozen burritos and Coke.

I sit in silence, remembering Weldon. Thinking about how if I'd met Drac back in high school, maybe we would have been honest friends, then. Like-minded. Maybe not exactly the same, but wanting similar things. I wasn't a sex addict back then. I wasn't a porn star. I was just a boy who was lonely. But would he have liked even the ugly me? I was real. I guess that counts for something, because I can see it in his eyes when he doesn't laugh. When Weldon Philbert is like the word *captain,* just another label.

I can't wait any longer. The energy between us is strong. He has to feel it. "Will you ever let me kiss you?"

"Will you ever show me one of your unpublished poems?" he counters.

My cheeks heat. At the kiss or the poem? I don't know which.

"But they're not the publishable ones. They're stupid."

"So you say. And the touching of lips is more than sex, but affection. That might be stupid, too. Depending on who it's with or what it means to them."

He has a way with words, but I didn't see it at first when he wasn't open. When he failed to talk much. But now? I love how he can hone in on depth of meaning, on the heart of a topic, which right now happens to be about our dating, our thing, our relationship if that's what it's becoming.

I sit very still. I can feel him staring at me.

"Are you not ready to share?" he asks.

I take a deep breath. I've taken my clothes off so many times in public I can't count. I've publicly fucked hundreds. I preen, I show off, I come for the camera. But this…

The cameras are rolling. Even here. In the ceiling, the bulkheads, the deck.

I get up and go to my desk. The folders are on my tablet under a lock and key.

When I return to the couch with my tablet, I open it. I log in with thumb print, retinal scan and a code.

My notebooks pop up. I see hundreds of poems by title and date. I don't really reread them much. I can't remember half of them. I tell myself they don't matter. They're about love. Not space. And I don't do that. Not in vids. Not for my brand. Not for fun. John Luke cured me of that. Until now.

I pick one, pop it up. Read a few lines at random. It's a credit to Drac that he doesn't move, doesn't try to read over my arm. It begins:

a boy dressed in wind
turning away from candlelight
the rippling soft tones
lips, pillow, new star

I close my eyes to more. I remember writing it. I was in a lonely mood. I don't usually get lonely. So it's kind of embarrassing.

I hand the screen over to Drac.

Eyes still closed, I feel him take it.

After about half a minute, I peek at him.

He is looking at me. "May I read some lines out loud?"

"No…" I shake my head. "Please."

He says, after reading silently, "It's beautiful."

"Okay, just three lines," I say. I'm not breathing. "Pick three."

He says, very softly, with a reverence in his tone like maybe he really is a trained actor, "Muses and houses and old shutters. Behind me a black poem. Ahead of me an alien lover."

He looks up at me.

"Am I still breathing?" I ask.

He nods, then he leans in. He puts his hand on the side of my face and moves his mouth to mine.

When his lips touch mine, a dry soft caress, my skin flames. He smells of storms and sunlight, known and unknown all at the same time. He holds his mouth against mine as if he is concentrating everything he is right there, feeling, just feeling.

His lips are full and lush. Trembling a little. Warm. His hand on my cheek cups gently, the fingertips pressing, the palm barely touching. His bangs tickle my forehead.

After a long moment, when things feel right, I puff my lips a little, giving him a kiss in return, though we have not yet parted. I open my mouth just enough to catch the skin of his upper lip between my own. He lets me do that twice before pulling away and taking a deep, loud breath.

I watch him, painfully hard, body taut and heated.

"Am I still breathing?" he asks.

I smile and nod.

"Stirling—I—you're different than I thought."

"You said that. I still don't know if it's a compliment, but I'll take it."

"It is," he assures me.

"That was really good. Now *I* want to kiss *you*."

His eyebrows are half-raised, his eyes wide open. In answer, he leans in.

Our second kiss sears me to the core. I swear I could come from just kissing him. I open my mouth more this time, and he does the same, latching us together deeper. Our tongues meet.

He tastes of the strawberry ice cream shakes we just ate, and of a deeper essence that my secret poems can't even contain. I've been searching for this feeling all my life without knowing it.

He lets me reach out and up, place my hand alongside his neck and slide to the back of his head. I pull him tighter to me. His mouth opens wider. His hand is flat on my chest but not to push me away. He's pressing his palm to my heartbeat. It's the gesture of a lover, not a porn star.

My body is on fire. I already want to kiss him all night long. Nothing else matters. He's amazing in so many ways, not just his beauty.

I'm disappointed when he pulls away for a breath.

"I want you," I whisper.

His face is flushed, pupils dilated. At his leather-bound crotch: a noticeable bulge. His gaze flickers. He looks from me to his bed through the archway from his office to his sleep space. I get up and grab his hands, pulling him to his feet. He comes willingly. His vest rides back revealing more of his chest. Perfectly muscled. Lean and tight.

His bed is covered with a plush spread the color of an ocean at noon. I wait for him to sit first, but he stands at the side of it looking down, chest rising and falling.

"Hey," I say. "It's your first mission. I know."

His mouth grimaces. He turns his head to the side as if to admonish me, but says nothing. I crave anything from him. Everything. Even admonishment would be fine. Just as long as he doesn't reject me. Not now.

"What I mean is," I try to clarify, "I've got your back. Nerves are common."

"Isn't it weird knowing all the cameras are around?"

"You get used to it. You forget about them. Let the editors worry about making it look like whatever they want it to be. We can just be."

"But of course you perform for the cameras," Drac insists.

"It's whatever you want. We're pros so yes we perform. But don't think about that right now." I want less talk and more of his incredible kissing. The moment is too sweet to lose to practicalities.

He holds back a little, shoulders hunching.

"You okay with this?" I ask, fearing the answer.

"I haven't done it live before."

"It's not really live. There's editing and final packaging even though it all seems like it happens overnight."

He nods.

"Didn't you audition?"

"On paper. And in an interview. There weren't cameras."

"None that you could see," I inform him with a smile.

"Oh."

"Come on." I tug his hands, which are a little slippery now. I pull him toward me and feel my thighs impact with the side of his mattress. I let my weight pull me down. He follows. I spread my legs and scoot back to make room for him.

He leans on his knees between my legs. I let go of his hands and wrap my arms around his shoulders. He is a force. At first he doesn't budge, but then he loosens up and lets himself bend over me, propping himself with his hands on either side of my shoulders. When he kisses me like that, my vision goes white.

His lips are firm and soft at the same time. His tongue is shy but strong, and I am so happy to report he is no slobbery kisser.

Slowly, Drac lowers his weight until I can feel his stomach against mine, and his definite hard-on. My hips rock, push up a little so he can feel me. In response, I receive a grunt and he kisses me harder.

My arousal flares even more, if possible, as if my entire body is one big erogenous zone.

His body feels big in my embrace, but also light, graceful. Sweet. My hands run down his back, under his vest to his waist. The naked skin is like satin. My hands want to feel more. My fingers caress between the "V" of his pants.

Drac pushes up, clutching at my shoulders and looks down at me, eyebrows narrowed.

"What?" I ask.

"Can we take this slow?"

His clothes are in the way, but I can wait. "Hell yeah."

I turn us on the bed until we are on our sides, face to face. I run a hand up over his side to his neck, his jaw, then through his shining hair. An erotic flame lights up his eyes.

The way to this man's heart is not through crudeness or quick, lascivious flirting. I understand this now. He's not a mere fuck-toy like me. He deserves more.

I stare into his eyes and it's a strange comfort. I'm hard and wanting and trembling, but getting off is not the first thing I'm thinking about in this moment. How odd.

He smiles. "You look rather perplexed."

I *love* the way he talks.

"Well?" he pushes.

"I like being with you. Going slow. Thank you for suggesting it."

"You mean yes, we can be boring for the cameras."

"You're not boring. And stop thinking about them. They shouldn't concern us right now."

He nods. His thick lashes flutter. I lean up and kiss him right below his left eye. I stream more kisses across to his temple, down his cheek, to his jaw line. I give a quick lick under his ear, then kiss my way down the side of his neck.

His hands hold tight to my waist, one trapped under my weight but still able to grip. My knee bends and finds its way between his legs. We embrace tighter and I bring my mouth again to his.

I love sex. I always have. But I have used it so much in a business sense I almost forgot how much more it can be. It's natural, of course, but to feel like you are sharing more than pleasure, to feel as if you want to be deeper with another, be a part of them, those feelings sweep over me and ramp up the thrill. This high with Drac is personal, and off the charts.

For a long time we stay like that, pressing, kissing. The bed cushions my shoulder and the side of my head. Drac is warm and encompassing. I bask in his nearness, his heat, his breath. I want more but at the same time I don't feel rushed. It's lovely how our groins push into each other with yearning, but we can still keep that height of pleasure without doing anything more.

Delayed gratification. I could be into that. But this is something else, something right and wonderful and perfect for no other reason than to be with each other on all levels.

Drac pulls back a little, cups my face, and pushes my perfectly styled hair back from my forehead. I feel my eyes roll up at the gentle gesture.

"You are quite engaging when you're not trying to be something you're not."

"Thank you, I think." Not sure if I should be insulted.

"I mean when you're just you, you're quite beautiful. Not that you're not all the time."

I grin. "I get it. You're talking about the parts that aren't a role."

"Yes."

"And you? Are you in a role?"

Instead of answering, he kisses me some more and I promptly forget the subject.

I decide to wait until Drac takes the lead for more. I've never waited so long in my life for someone to disrobe me. After about a half-hour of clothed foreplay, he moves up in the bed and tugs at my tie and the buttons on my shirt.

I help him get those things off me, then reach for his vest. It's so soft in my hands, so light, but I throw it overboard.

Naked chest to naked chest, we spend more minutes getting used to each other again. I can feel his heart beat against me. His exhales are warm in my hair, on my neck, and against my upper peck.

He takes his time exploring my chest. I love it. My nipples are diamond hard. He kisses the left one, his lips barely brushing. My whole body feels it. It's as if I'm levitating right off the bed and for a moment I wonder if the ship has lost its artificial gravity.

Drac's tongue, like velvet, brushes over my nipple, and a few seconds later the dampness of that kiss zings through me as the air touches it making it almost cold. He licks again.

I don't think I've ever come just from someone licking my nipples.

I don't know if I'll survive this. I'm used to play-book fucking with a few kinks thrown in. With Drac, that book is burned to ash.

I cry out as he sucks my nipple into his mouth.

He pulls back. "Okay?"

"Fuck, yes!"

He chuckles. "You're the experienced one. Just checking."

"Yeah. More, please."

He takes his time, giving lots of attention to my nipples. At long last he works his way down my flat belly, kissing and licking. I can't stop my body from arching up.

He meets my eyes as his fingers fumble with my waistband button. My jeans are tight. The bulge below is quivering, pressing hard at the material. I can feel the dampness of my arousal.

I lift up and tug at the back of my jeans, scooting out of them. My cock bobs free as I push my jeans down my thighs and all the way off. I have this weird sensation of vulnerability that is not normal for me. I laugh it off and turn, bending my knees.

Drac's hand presses my stomach just above where my cock stretches up. He doesn't gawk at it. Instead, he looks down at me, eyes smiling, and runs his hand to the side and down my naked hip. Everything I am and perhaps may ever be begins to tremble.

"I love how you touch me," I say.

"You are quite—um—gorgeous. To say the least."

I yank on his own waistband, which is easy because of the "V" cuts in the front and back of his pants. His pants are very loose and only cling to him because they are slightly stiff leather. There is a small set of buttons behind a flap at his groin. Those are tight, right against his bulge. I need to sit up. I need both hands.

He says, "Lie back. I'll do it." His voice rumbles through me.

When Drac's leathers come off and he's naked, I am stunned even more by his beauty. He's perfect in every way, how the skin at his hips dents, the way it curves over the muscles of his thighs, dark and gleaming in the low light of the bedroom, and his beautiful cock, dark at the shaft but pink-tipped, throbbing upward. The head pushes past the foreskin, shining.

I press myself against him, feeling our bodies meet in shared heat, and kiss him for a long time. I can't get enough of that. Normally I'd just want to move on to the main event. But this—this is special. And I refuse to push him past anything he isn't ready himself to initiate.

But Drac is ready. I feel his hand rove down to my ass, caressing, squeezing. I arch into his grip. His other hand is trapped between us, with mine, and it pushes for enough space to caress me low, lower. My own hand follows his, over his taut abdomen, down to feel the firmness of his cock nudge my thigh, my fingers. My free hand is still on his shoulder, gripping as if I need balance.

I am dizzy. Reeling from him. His scent, his touch, his energy. The intermittent hum of his voice. The groans.

I grasp his cock and stroke up. A sharp inhale and he holds his breath, eyes shut.

From so much foreplay, we are both close. His hand grasps my own dick and instantly my euphoria begins the climb. Up and up. Everything threatening to blank out. Nothing real but this. No ship. No Solar System. No galaxy. Nothing but this and him. Drac. In my arms. In my hands.

It is as if he is stroking every fiber of my being. Up and down. Liquid drips down. My body thrums. He's thrumming, too, in my palm.

My body seeks its center and my mind moves outward.

I still have enough awareness to run the tips of my fingers over his balls, keep up my own caresses. They've already drawn up. He's about to explode. I stroke up and down, fast now. He echoes my movements and my cock pulses deep inside. My balls tingle. My body arches.

We both cry out. I'm coming and he is, too. His hand comes up from my ass and presses at the center of my back. Lips crash into mine, searing.

We come together stroking each other into the aftermath as if we've done it hundreds of times before. As if our bodies already know each other—were meant to be.

I never want this to end.

We pull apart. Our hands come up between us and clasp. We catch our breaths, staring at each other.

A voice inside my head keeps repeating. *Please tell me we're not done. Please tell me we're not done.*

My hand is wet. The dampness between us glues us together. I don't care. He doesn't care.

Drac pushes me over until I'm on my back. He lies on top of me. For the first time I see him grin.

I wrap my arms around him. Tight.

"More?" he asks in a whisper.

I nod. "More."

His grin catches mine as we continue to kiss as ship's night deepens.

Chapter Eight

We take few breaks our first night together. Only for dozing. Not for water or washing or any real sleep.

Drac moves like a dancer in bed. Everywhere at once. Making me his. Giving himself to me.

The first time I suck him into my mouth, he gushes with little warning.

"Weldon," he whispers, making my horrible real name sound like a prayer. Then louder, "Weldon!" And I hold him through the orgasm until he stops shaking.

He's not a virgin, but I can tell he's not super experienced, either. To me, he's perfect. He's the lover of my dreams.

I don't mind that he uses my old name. I know why. He's connecting to me. Not to Captain Stirling Kane. Not to some character I'm playing in a script. But to *me.*

Occasionally throughout the night, I remind myself of my personal promise I made: Don't let this become another John Luke.

But Drac is nothing like John Luke. I tell myself that over and over. He's warm and gentle and attentive. He is able to take charge, but he isn't in charge, if that makes any sense.

He might have ignored me at first, played hard to get, but he's not cool like John Luke was, keeping everything between us tidy and in its place. He's shy but open. Hair messy in his eyes. Sheepish smiles that pull his lower lip in between his teeth. And he asked to read one of my personal poems I have never shown a soul. John Luke would never have asked me that.

We doze and make love until morning. We don't really sleep. But I feel like we have slept together, and *slept* together and the intimacy between us is something I have not felt or thought of wanting in years.

Because I was hurt by my love for John Luke, I did not allow myself to realize how deeply intimacy is missing from my life.

I'm not necessarily an idiot, but I have let myself get caught up in unreal roles over the years, and played them well without any deeper self involvement.

When ship's morning arrives, we both declare we are starved.

Drac lets me use his sonic bath first. I dress again in my jeans, white shirt and tie.

When I come out of the bathroom, Drac is ready to go in.

"I'll wait for you," I say.

"No need. I'll meet you in the galley."

All right, I won't push it. I nod and leave him to his privacy.

On my walk to the mess hall, I'm floating. My eyes are slightly blurred from lack of sleep, yet I'm still euphoric. But my stomach begins to flutter with nerves again. I have just had the best night of my life in… ever. Now, being apart from Drac with my mind clearing a little, I am afraid.

Afraid I won't feel that ever again. Afraid Drac may not feel the same.

How can I be so unsure as I remember his sweet touches, his body so natural, so entwined with mine?

We did not actually fuck. Which is unheard of for a porn script. But this wasn't a script. Intercourse was nothing we ever thought of as we touched and made love. But I want that, too. I'm nervous because it was one night, and what if things end before they start?

In the galley I make two plates of eggs. Scrambled. Easy and light. I pour orange juice.

Others come in and out of the mess hall to eat. Armstrong remarks about my attire. "You look good. Formal and all."

"Thank you."

I keep the eggs under a warmer, hoping it's not too long before Drac arrives or they'll be like rubber.

I do not sit. I walk about the room. I go to the huge viewport and fiddle with the picture, giving it a purple screen.

Armstrong tries to engage me in light conversation, but stops when he sees I'm not listening.

I try not to look at the time, which ticks by at the bottom right corner of the viewer. It's been fifteen minutes. That's not long, I tell myself. It's nothing. He'll come.

Five more minutes go by. I'll need to make fresh eggs now. I think about adding toast to the meal this time.

My hands are shaking as I go to throw away the eggs, which are still steaming, still look good.

I hear the hiss of the mess hall door open and turn.

Drac enters. Alone. He's wearing jeans not unlike mine, and a sheer black tank. His hair is pulled back in a loose tail, casual but very neat. His eyes scan the room and stop on me.

"Hungry?" I ask.

"Starving," he replies and walks toward the table.

Armstrong observes this, as do a few of the others, with raised eyebrows. Drac is so aloof with them all. For him to come right to me gives everything away. I don't care. Drac is here. And all my blurred vision clears.

I take the eggs and serve them up.

"Toast?" I ask.

"Yes."

It's done in a minute and I bring the steaming plates over to the table and sit across from him. He has already drunk half his orange juice.

My hands are still shaking but he says nothing. Armstrong sighs, looking a bit dejected, gets up and leaves.

If there are others still milling about, eating, I don't see them. Drac is my whole world right now.

"I would have made bacon, too, but the supply on this mission sucks so bad. No one eats it."

"I heard." He puts a forkful of eggs into his mouth and chews. "Good."

"Thanks."

"Thanks for making breakfast."

"Thanks for last night."

And here we sit, thanking each other. Can you say *awkward*?

I start to laugh, as I often do when I'm unsure of myself. He laughs right along with me. In that, we're the same. It relaxes me to know this.

Everything is soft-focused right now. The food sparks in my mouth. Drac looks made of light and shadow, blue, black, bronze. I think I could fall into him forever.

I am starved and wolf my food. I pour us coffee. Someone else made it before I came in but there's plenty and it's good. I watch Drac put two creams and two sugars in his.

I like it with one cream. Slightly bitter.

After breakfast, I invite Drac to walk the ship with me. He's delighted.

"I've been wanting a real tour. I want to see things more close up."

"You can ask me anything you want about the ship. Not sure I'll have all the answers, but I've been with her for five years."

I am unsure, though. I want him to want to be with me, not look at the ship. My suggestion for a walk is an excuse just to be together. But I am glad to have his company.

In the corridor, I want to hold his hand but refrain. I'm such a sap. That is not normal for me!

And gods he has questions! So many questions. As I told him, I can only answer some of them, and only those because I've been doing this for so long.

Sometimes knowledge rubs off whether you want it to or not. It's not like I went to school for ship's diagnostics, or design. Or even the daily running of a ship. I follow scripts when it's called for. We don't have lines with much scientific jargon. It's more about someone's tight ass. Or fashion, make up, hair, lube and such for the individual sponsors who pay a lot for us to wear and use their stuff.

Still, I do my best to while showing him around.

Drac takes his time on the engineering level. I hope it's because maybe he wants to get me into a shadowed alcove. To my disappointment, he doesn't. But just being near him... that's all I need right now.

We spend a lot of the day exploring *Lacrosse* and he knows things even I don't know. It's not usual with my crew, but when I ask him about how he knows so much he says he likes to read. That's a fine hobby. Some paint. Some crochet. Some do crosswords. The ones who talk politics usually don't last. Most of them, when they're done commercializing themselves, or using a sponsored product, watch vids, play in vids, or do their nails. The most popular are into cute cat holos and flattering their fans.

I have to say in all my twenty-five years doing this job, five of which I've been the captain, I've never given any one of my fellow actors, detailed tour of the ship. Most wouldn't know a pressure sensor from a proximity sensor. Not even sure I do.

Drac touches bulkheads. Splays his hands over light grids. His whole being seems to pulse as if alive after a long sleep. I mean, he pulsed for me, in more ways than one. But if possible, he is even more attentive, excited.

When he starts talking about things I don't understand, I remain silent. Armstrong's gossip that there is a scientist aboard is probably right. But he's an amateur one. Nothing wrong with that. And I'm still determined to keep my mouth shut about it.

After lunch, I am longing for a nap.

I invite Drac but he declines, saying he needs to nap, too. "Really sleep," he says with a smirk.

I go back to my quarters alone.

My body wants to wind down but I have a hard time falling asleep. My skin tingles with the memory of Drac's touch. I grab a pillow and pull it tight to my chest, as if I am holding him against me. I've bathed, but it's as if I can still smell him on my arms, my legs, as if I can taste him on my lips.

Finally, darkness sweeps over me, peaceful and welcoming.

Chapter Nine

My dreams are liquid. Echoing. Soft. I don't remember them coherently, but there are shapes and textures and stars.

I wake feeling strangely hollow but refreshed. I drink a lot of water.

I go over some emails from the PTB. Mostly they are about what the crew are doing, and if they are even remotely on script.

Everything is fine. There is nothing from PTB about my performance last night with Drac. Perhaps they haven't gotten to it yet. Usually they are so quick.

I look up our ratings. Nothing has changed. Yet. By tomorrow maybe. Then we'll see how the audience likes our pairing. Me and Drac together.

I sign off on a few things to do with sponsors. I see there is a note about a script change, but it's not for any time in the next few days so I make a note to look it over later.

My fingers ache to look up Drac's name, go deeper into hidden files. I don't do it. I should get a medal, I think. But I'm no stalker. And he'll tell me what he wants to tell me as we get closer.

I hope that will happen.

We have another dinner date which I arranged. This time on the observation deck. I have a whole picnic planned out under the stars. What could be better? Space is the perfect place for that.

I finish my correspondence as Captain, and arrive at the galley with plenty of time to put together a basket of goodies for us.

Danielle is there, finishing a meal. She's gorgeous in a hot pink bikini top and lace skirt. She looks up at me, her face perfectly made up. I wonder who she's meeting later. But her stare turns to a glare. It's not a friendly gaze now.

"Don't hurt my brother," she says.

"What?"

"Don't. He's new. He's sensitive, okay?"

"Okay." I frown. "It's not my intention to hurt anyone. And I like Drac." More than *like,* says a low voice in my head.

"Sure." She says it like she doesn't believe it. "He's not hard like we are. He's not seasoned."

"I know that. I'm not some monster. I can be kind and gentle."

She makes a disgusted noise. "You're the playboy of the stars."

"Is that what they call me now?" I laugh.

"No. It's what I call you behind your back."

The muscles around my eyes tighten. I turn away. I can't think of any comeback to that. Sure, we crew can get into fights. Even I do, as the captain, when I forget for a moment my role is supposed to inspire cooperation, camaraderie, but I don't deserve this rudeness from her. I reassure myself she's just looking out for her brother. She's being the protective big sister. He told me himself she is like that.

Finally, I say, my back still to her, "I'm meeting him again tonight. Is that okay with you?"

I hear a noise like a quick *humf.*

"We get along well." I turn, the full basket in my hand. "I hope to be seeing a lot of him on this voyage."

"I know. He's into you. He told me but he didn't have to. And half the crew knows. All those moony looks you gave each other today. The ship tour. People talk."

"I know." Our version of the corporate water cooler. Gossip on this ship flies fast and hard.

"Well? What's going on? You can tell me."

I shrug. "Hanging out again tonight."

"He's that good, eh?"

Normally, I'd always say yes. About any of my crew. We have an honor code among each other. We don't critique each other's work. Ever. But I don't feel like treating Drac as just any other crew member. I say, "I already told you. We get along well."

When I pick up the basket and head for the door, her gaze follows me. The smirk has still not left her face.

*

When I arrive at the upper deck I spy Drac already sitting on the long lounge facing the viewport. I set the basket on the floor and fall back beside him.

The viewport takes up the entire bulkhead. There's usually not much to see but darkness, but it seems Drac has the settings altered to give a little color and magnify the stars. This port does not face Earth, so there is no tiny blue star to try to find out there.

I don't miss home. Not yet. But sometimes on the longer voyages, I cannot wait to be planet-side in fresh air and real gravity, maybe sit on my porch and listen to the crickets. My money has bought me a nice place in Big Bear, east of Los Angeles. It's shady and peaceful, and in winter it snows, which is amazing. I love my real wood fire place.

I reach into the basket. "I have wine coolers this time. Sorry I couldn't find any Coke."

"No problem." But one sleek eyebrow rises.

"Are you hungry?"

"It seems I have been all day today."

"Yeah. Staying up all night will do that to a body."

He gives a quick laugh.

I bring out the wine-cooler bottles and some sandwiches. Drac looks pleased.

Immediately, Drac starts telling me about how amazing *Lacrosse* is as we eat. His excitement is contagious.

We finish eating and relax. He is more talkative than ever. I never thought I'd see it.

Finally, I find an opening to speak. I'm so enamored I can only think of one thing. "Will you kiss me again?"

He leans forward, eyes alight. "Will you spend the night with me again?"

"Yes!"

We end up in my quarters this time.

We can't undress fast enough. When we fall into bed, it's as if we never got up this morning. Everything resumes as if we never stopped making love. Our bodies press. Our lips merge. My hands and his hands explore everywhere. Our mouths follow.

My orgasms break me apart. I am totally infatuated. Damn him, I'm in love.

I want him everywhere. On me. In me. I offer myself and he accepts by way of taking the lube I grab from my bedside cabinet.

He is thorough and gentle with me, more so than any other lover I've ever had. Correction. They were not lovers. They were business partners. Hook ups for the cameras, for the masses to view and get off on.

It's not like that with Drac. He takes his time. I'm on my hands and knees, and he doesn't thrust into me like an overzealous actor. He goes slow so the burn is almost non-existent. I'm stretched, but his patience lets me feel myself stretch further in pure pleasure.

When his hips graze my ass, he reaches around me and holds me tight to him, the embrace adding to the connection, the affection I can feel throbbing inside me, starting the euphoria to begin its roll through me.

I press back into him, trying to get him deeper. I am filled to the brim, mind, heart and ass. I want him there forever.

I moan.

Drac says my name. "Stirling. Weldon. You feel incredible."

"You can move," I say.

He starts to pull back. Everything is slick and I don't feel the usual uncomfortable sensation as I get used to the thrusts. He pushes in again, slow and gentle.

"You can go faster," I assure him.

He laughs. He hugs me tighter to him. "I just want to feel you for a minute."

"That's okay."

I let my head fall forward on my pillow. Voice muffled now, ass in air, I say, "What's your real name?"

"It's Drac. My parents were emo or Goths or whatever you call it."

He pulls out again and thrusts back in a little harder. "Oh! That's good!"

No more talk. Just great thrusting. He's so hard. Such a perfect fit. And the way it's so smooth and natural, as if our bodies are meant to be one, is truly making love.

He must feel what I'm feeling. I can't be wrong about this. His shining eyes, his eagerness to spend the whole night with me last night, and now this.

We get into a rhythm and I never want to stop.

My cock is so hard it's flat against my belly. Pre-cum leaks from the tip and dribbles down. The head catches on my spread. It will leave a stain but I'm used to it. I've left more stains and washed more coverlets and sheets in a year than most people do in their lives. Yeah, I've had that much sex.

But this beats it all.

Drac's thrusting becomes more interesting. Faster, yes, but he spins his hips a little and now the head of his cock is hitting my prostate every time he pushes back in. It causes little explosions in my mind, white and pink and red, and my blood burns.

My whole body is charged with bliss. It's already so good I could die happy like this. But when he pulls back and runs his hands over my waist, down my thighs, gripping, one hand encasing my cock, the climb to even greater ecstasy begins.

I can't stop moaning. No control. Not that I want it.

Drac strokes my cock to the rhythm of his thrusts, faster and faster. We have wings now. We have lift-off.

I go up and up until it seems there is no *up* left. But somehow there is, and I go even higher. Drac is keeping me poised on the precipice of utter rapture. His cries mingle with mine.

I reach back and grab his hip, pulling him tight against me. "Come with me. Come with me," I yell, because I don't think I can hold back any longer and still live.

Everything is colors out the corners of my eyes, and the perfumed fragrance of union. It's all flying and rolling through the sweetest desire I've ever experienced. I slide my legs wider, trying to get him closer, deeper. He hits that spot again. Again. One more time and I'm lost. Falling. Screaming. Heaven explodes into a million heavens. I hear Drac crying out as if from a distance. Calling my name. "Stirling. Weldon."

I don't care what he calls me. As long as he is with me. As long as he holds on and we do this together, I'll be exhilarated forever.

*

When I come out of my bathroom, Drac is sound asleep. The covers are bunched about his feet and thighs, and he's curled into a pillow. His back and ass are revealed, all the long muscle sweeps and dips brushed with shadow and light. I moved onto the bed, curling up behind him, my arm going around his waist. His buttocks press against my thighs. My chest rubs his back. His breathing changes slightly and he pushes himself back. I embrace him tighter, bow my head until my nose parts the hair at the base of his neck, and close my eyes.

I have never spent two nights in a row with anyone. Even John Luke would kick me out of his bed despite a perceived intimacy I thought we had for each other, despite my love for him.

I want Drac with me all the time now. Is this just me acting like a kid again?

But my body doesn't think. It knows. Something deeper than flesh and porn-star thoughts craves him.

As I fall to sleep, I am thinking: *What will happen after this mission? What am I going to do?*

Chapter Ten

For the next week, Drac and I take all our meals together. We spend every night in each other's arms. We try out every position we can think of. We take turns topping and bottoming. We both confess we can't decide which we like best. It's a testament to our talents.

Or maybe it's more. I like to think that. Love plays a part, most definitely. I say, *I love you* in my mind a hundred times a day.

But neither of us has said it aloud.

The rest of the crew ignores us.

The script is more like an outline. Not a rule. It doesn't tell us who we are supposed to have relationships with, or for how long. We all play it by what feels right in the moment. So everyone assumes Drac and I are feeling *right*. At the moment. No one suspects it's anything more.

Except Danielle.

Danielle glowers sometimes in passing, but Drac always smiles at her, and she forces him into conversations. She pretty much ignores me, which wasn't the way when all this started. I don't know if she hates that Drac is with me all the time now or if she wants more of his attention or what.

This morning, in the galley, after Danielle talks to Drac and leaves, Drac comes up to me and says, "Dani says I have fan mail I'm ignoring." He shrugs. "Who knew?"

"Right. I pretty much ignore that. I never watch my own vids."

"No?"

I shake my head. "It makes me self-conscious. I just can't."

"Anyway, I have some work to do today in my quarters."

I understand that he's trying to say, nicely, that he's taking a break.

I have work, too, that I've been neglecting. "I'm backlogged in my own reports. The PTB likes to hear from me now and then. I've been ignoring their messages."

"We can meet for lunch," Drac offers.

I lean up and kiss him. "Good plan."

Once in my quarters and at my computer, I realize how much I've been neglecting what few duties I have other than playing my role and fucking my crew. My agent has left ten messages. The PTB at least that many. And my PR rep has left me two. The last two usually have to do with promotional stuff and public appearances when I am on Earth so I ignore them for now.

I deal with all of it as quickly as I can. The PTB sends me daily reports on my crew. Because I am Captain, if any of them aren't doing well in their ratings, or are having problems settling, mixing, or the fans hate what they're wearing, etc., they get a message and I get a message. I follow up with them while at the same time try not to micromanage them. I'm their boss in space, but their real bosses are the PTB. They own the rights to everything. They are the corporation we work for.

When I receive the report on Drac, everything seems fine. Apparently our first vid was a mega hit. We are ranked in the top ten. He's actually ahead of me. Jealousy flares for only a second and is gone. I'm so proud of him. But another short message pops up beside the first. Like a postscript.

Drac has a lot of computer activity but we don't see him at his computer enough to account for it. If he has auto-responses to his fan mail, that might account for some of it. But some of his outgoing messages are in terabytes. Look into this. I see you have access now. Could be a computer glitch.
--Bill Trastivor, PTB

Bill is the guy who corresponds with me the most. He's like my handler from the corporation. Mostly, if the PTB has questions about a crew member, I meet with them, we go over the problem and solve it or not. If not, sometimes that crew member is fired when we return to Earth.

But this is different. Like spying. I don't recall doing that before.

As Captain, I have access to files and parts of the ship's computer the rest of the crew doesn't have. Some of it is considered sensitive and encrypted. I never need to access that stuff.

I also have access to personal interactions on all computers on board. But I don't look at that stuff. Ever. There was only one time I had to, and that was when one of my crew was illegally selling bootleg vids of himself in space on the darkweb market. I didn't have to do much in that case. The PTB cut him off from all media when they caught him. I confiscated his tech. That was it. He was pissed but stayed to himself until we got back to Earth. Not sure what happened to him after that.

I pull up Drac's accounts. I feel spacesick just doing that. I love him and now I'm intruding on his personal stuff.

I tell myself I'm just going to glance at it all and see that it's fine. Then I will return a quick message to Bill at PTB that everything's in order.

But when I look, everything isn't in order.

I can't see what it is, and I should be able to, but Drac's been sending a lot heavily loaded messages back to Earth to something called Vistech. It can't be right.

I check again. I see chunks of information outgoing. But I am blocked from seeing what it is.

My computer messages me that its system on the bridge has a program I can use to see more. Why can't the PTB do this from their end? Why does it have to be me?

I send a quick message off to Bill asking him to do it from their end.

I do other work while waiting for a reply.

Two hours later I receive it.

Drac's accounts are blocked from us. He's used the ship's systems themselves to block us. There's an auto-reroute of our attempts to break through. If you can get in through the bridge system manually and follow its instructions, maybe you can find out more.

Bill Trastivor, PTB

Because Drac's system is wired through the ship, that's now the only way in. PTB does not have the override options I might have if I use voice command on the bridge.

I'm not a damn computer geek. I don't know what I'm doing. And all of this is freaking me out. Drac is my lover. I don't want to know that he's doing anything wrong. I don't want to be the one to catch him.

If he's selling bootleg vids or anything like that, I don't want to know.

I spend another hour pacing my quarters, wishing I had my lucky gold coin back so I can juggle it across my knuckles. That always soothes me.

But Drac has it. And I want him to have it. I want to feel his arms around me. I want to go to him and tell him about all this, have him tell me there's an easy and logical explanation. That nothing is wrong.

With a huff, I grab my tablet and head to the bridge.

Chapter Eleven

When I get to the bridge, as expected it is empty. No one needs to be there, so they hardly ever are. There are a lot of screens and lights. The floor is hard. There are chairs at various stations, and a bigger, softer captain's chair. I've had sex there many times. The bridge isn't used for much else.

There is one section of the bridge which isn't just a model for the set, though. It contains a readout screen, as well as access to PTB library computers back on Earth. I never take advantage of this access. I don't want more knowledge than I need to do my job. It just complicates things.

I have the password. Just in case. But now I have to use my code for a way in to access Drac's personal account.

I verbally open the program. I speak my private code aloud. "Zero zero zero zero one."

First, before I look at Drac's activity again and try to see what he's exporting, I can't stop myself from checking on his personal PTB bio. I set it for reading since I can read twice as fast as the computer talks. Just that small process gives me a headache. Not because it's work, but because it's Drac.

Immediately, I see both Drac and Danielle's files. Why? Hers must be connected to his and I open it. It's the standard file, though. Nothing much that I didn't already know about her.

It is less than suspicious. If she's a scientist, then she's been undercover as a Hero for ten years. This is her twenty-second mission – first time under my command – and she likes to read. Because of her beauty, she's a popular crewer, but her love of the classics bores viewers. As with all Heroes, she's bisexual.

PTB thought that with her closeness to her younger brother, Drac, she might climb the popularity chart. They are hoping there might be some incest on the side. I know now there isn't, but her record lists it as a factor in ratings and the possibility this could be exploited. In one month her rank has gone from one hundred and four to forty-four.

Drac's file follows.

I scroll down to his popularity rating. I'd meant to look it up in my quarters, but forgot. I rarely look at my own. Usually I don't care about numbers. They don't affect my performance. Last I looked, we were both in the top ten. But that was days ago.

When I see Drac is number two, right below John-Luke who is always number one, and two above me — I'm at four? — I do a double-take. We are both climbing fast. A thrill at this success courses through me.

I verbally command the computer to show me Drac's transactions for the past week from *Lacrosse* to Earth.

Coincidentally, Drac chooses that moment to walk onto the bridge.

I turn and my eyes must still be registering shock, because he says, not meeting my eyes, "Are you all right?"

"Sure," I sputter. "Just fine. What are you doing here?"

He looks at the screen on the console before me just before I deftly flick it off, then walks past me toward the main viewer.

"What are you doing here? Looking at the view?"

It's like he didn't see me with the computer console on. Good. "Uh, yeah. I like to hang out up here sometimes."

"Playing the captain's role to the hilt?"

I don't like how that sounds but it's true. "I guess."

Drac wears black Levis with the seat missing halfway down his crack and exposing the tops of the backs of his thighs, no underwear, and a mesh gold shirt. His black, old-fashioned cowboy boots click like hammers against the deck.

"When you gave me the tour up here, you didn't show me everything, did you?" he asks. His shoulder-length hair is haloed by the bluish viewport light.

"What do you mean *everything*?" I get up and go to my chair in the center of the bridge, leaning against it. I move around the armrest to sit in it. He's so handsome. It distracts me and all I can think is how much I want him and what the fuck is going on because he's acting suddenly weird.

Half-blocked blue light surrounds him as he shifts in front of the viewport, barely turning. His face is in profile now as he glances out the corner of his eye at me leaning on my captain's altar.

He laughs. "You know the computer systems on this ship are limited in order to monitor and maintain the areas they are situated in. All except the computer on the bridge which links everywhere, even to Earth. And responds to your voice commands overriding even the most complicated blocks."

My skull is throbbing now. "I do know that. But I never use this system up here. I don't need to. And I didn't show it to you because there's nothing to it. Nothing to see."

"Nothing to see. But… you were accessing it just now." He laughs.

Something deep inside me sinks. When I don't return the laugh, he comes over and hunkers at my feet. He's seems more rough-hewn, gangly now that he's sorta scaring me. And even more totally my type. His dark eyes are harder, chipped onyx. His mouth, when it smiles at me, doesn't curve. I'm used to it. I've had that mouth all over my body. I want that again, but something's not right here.

As he looks at me without blinking, for a moment I have the queasy feeling he hates me. He knows what I've been doing. Spying on him. But if he has nothing to hide, why should he be bothered?

His long fingers touch my leather-tucked knee. "How about we go back to your quarters?"

Sounds great. "Yeah. But I just wanted a little time up here alone. You know? Meet you in half an hour?"

A little time alone up here. Why did I say that? Oh gods, that sounds so stupid. Where's a real script when you need one?

"You want to spend time here pretending you're really the one in charge?"

It sounds like an insult. I refuse to take it as one.

I lean forward and kiss him on the lips. I want him. My gut aches with want. He's number two in the ratings. Nothing should fuck with that. I shouldn't fuck with that.

When I pull back I notice he's carefully watching me. Too careful.

Why am I doing this? I don't care what Drac is up to. Let PTB handle it all when we get home. It's not in the script. And I am not the FBI. I'm the captain, damn it. And it's just not in me to be anything like a real hero, small "h."

I press my hand between my eyes. "You know, I've changed my mind. I want you. Now. In my quarters."

But something inside me is like warning bells going off. Armstrong's words come back to me. *There's a rumor....* A voice in my head, trying to be heard over my self-criticism at my conflicted position, keeps saying, *What if he's really a scientist?*

The starlight seems to surge as I rise to my feet. He doesn't move. When I try to step past him, Drac reaches out so fast to grab my ankle that I have no time to respond. He pulls my foot out from under me and I topple backwards to the hard deck, whacking my head on the gilded captain's throne.

"Star-shit! What'd you do that for?" My vision swims. My voice, strained with shock, comes out strangled. He straddles me and grabs both my wrists.

"You know, don't you?" His face fills my view.

"Drac! What the fuck?"

There's a glimmer of moisture on the corner of his mouth. Is this the same Drac I'm in love with?

"I saw you accessing my file from my computer in my quarters. Who'd you talk to? What's the plan? To dump me at Jupiter? Gas me in my sleep?"

His hands drop mine and go for a tight grip on my throat. By this time I'm bucking like a star wrestler, trying to throw him off. I don't think about the royalties for this play. I don't think about the awards. It's life that precious to a Hero. Life first. Then the stars. Then sex. Is Drac a bootlegger? A scientist?

And why the ever-loving fuck does he think I want to kill him?

"What the fuck." I cough as his hand tightens.

"You know everything. Damn you!"

"Can't breathe," I say, retching, pushing at his wrists.

"What were you going to do to me?" he yells, banging my head against the deck. "Was it all a ploy? You get close to me, get to know me, try to get information on me being a scientist?"

The admission, after all this, still surprises me.

I see tears start in the corners of his eyes.

He's bigger than me, stronger, but I'm a Hero. Primed for this. I've got twenty-five years experience on him and a still-young body myself. I work out four days a week.

I push hard enough to get him off-balance. His grip loosens and I fling him with all my strength to one side, kicking at his bent legs in the process. I pummel his face with my fists and red blood flows from his nose. His skull knocks against the captain's chair and that really slows him down.

I grab his shoulders, shake. His dark head lolls. "Until now, it was your sister I suspected, you idiot. And there is no plan! I fucking love you!"

"Screw me," he says, and as most folks do after taking a Hero's punch direct in the face, he passes out.

*

"I say we grease the rat-fucked son of a bitch!" Armstrong dramatically makes his bejeweled hand into a fist.

"Oh quit quoting famous classics, Arm. You're boring," Hunter complains. She's lounging on a table, eating dehydrated fudge. Thick brown hair hangs in her face. Her right bare foot rests on Drac's gold-mesh-covered shoulder. The shirt is stained brown in front from the nosebleed I gave him.

At the table, facing away from Hunter and toward the rest of us, Drac Blacque sits tied to a chair. A blue silk scarf gags him. Every time Hunter's toes tickle his cheek, he rolls his eyes, very Danielle-like.

Danielle, in the far corner, watches, cheeks tear-streaked. So far, she's said nothing.

"We're not going to grease anyone," I say, watching my captive's reaction. I mean, we don't do that out here in space. In worst case scenarios, we have a brig where someone can stay and cool off until the PTB decides whether to involve authorities when we return to Earth.

Drac's nose shows signs of a mottled, purple bruise. His eyes are the same hard darkness. Up to now, he's revealed no emotion.

I, on the other hand, have been fighting back tears, sitting with my knees tucked up to my chest in a chair at the head of the table. *Drac hates me. Drac tried to kill me.* I cannot get those thoughts out of my mind.

"Why not?" Sigourney Quinn asks. Her hobby is dance, and she's very good at it. "He attacked the captain. That's a capital offense."

"Yeah," Shariff Parque, *Lacrosse*'s vague excuse for a doctor – though he's more talented at spacewalking – adds. "He tried to kill you."

"You guys are so stupid. You're still just thinking of your ratings. All of you!" I get up from my chair and stalk over to Drac.

I watch the chiseled brown eyes. For a moment I think I see fear spark them. "Maybe he was afraid for his life," I say.

"What?" Hunter's chocolate-smeared lips scowl.

"Maybe he thought I knew about him and was going to kill him." That's what he told me on the bridge, but that's stupid. If he had done his research on me, he would know I've never killed anyone in my life. I wouldn't start with my own lover. He has to know that.

Drac watches me with a piqued interest. His dark brows rise slightly.

Darcy Chance, dressed all in black and the best singer on board, says quietly, "He's entitled to a fair trial."

Is that the script? Is that what we're going to do now?

Danielle steps forward. Despite the tears, her voice is strong. "How can it be fair? He's entitled to a jury of his peers and there's none on this ship. We're all Heroes. His I.Q. is higher than all of us put together."

Everyone turns and stares at her.

"Are you really a scientist, Drac? Really?" Sigourney asks. Her black eyes glower as she turns to Danielle. "You've been protecting him all this time!"

"I didn't know about Drac! He's a little shy, that's all. Always has been since he was a kid. I wanted to help him settle in, protect him. All my family are Heroes. But now, now that we know the truth, that he's a scientist," she spits the words, "that's no reason to...to...kill him! Come on, you guys. Why are we even using that word."

But she gives him a look as if he's been hiding secrets from her their whole lives, and she's hurt, too.

I can't help but feel sorry for her. If it weren't for her true devotion to her brother, he might never have had the courage to come aboard. We would never have met.

"No one's killing anyone. And I think Danielle's telling the truth," I say.

"She's arguing to spare his life," Armstrong says, nodding.

"Life. A Hero's first priority," Shariff says.

The others reluctantly agree.

"Well, he's one of us, too," I say, pointing a shaking finger at Drac. "He passed all the tests to get here."

Danielle gives me a relieved look and comes to stand beside me. "Thank you."

"Well." I glance down at her. "What do you suggest we do?"

Danielle looks up at me, blinks away tears and says, "Let him speak." She turns toward her brother. "He'll tell me the truth. And if he's working for anyone, we need to find out."

"He didn't tell anyone the truth before," Armstrong mutters under his breath.

"Take the gag off." I nod at Hunter. She puts down her fudge and scoots across the table on her ass. Her hands undo the silk scarf and free his mouth. She uses it to tie up her heavy hair, then goes back to her fudge.

Drac coughs, licks his lips.

Danielle says to Drac, "If you cooperate, maybe they'll go easier on you back on Earth?"

Drac rolls his eyes and gives a pained laugh.

"You're laughing now?" I ask. I start to get in his face, then turn away. I don't want him to see the new tears that start to blur my vision.

"What were you going to do, Drac?" Danielle asks softly.

He looks away.

"Drac?"

"None of you can understand."

"Try us," I say. "Are you working for someone? What's the end game?"

Drac lets out a forced sigh. "Do you realize that for eighty years space travel has been stagnant? Nothing's changed. Oh, you bring back samples, but any computer could do that. You do Hollywood stunts like spacewalking and spacefucking, but what does that teach us? Not one byte of information we couldn't get on our own. You're not Heroes. You don't take risks. You don't break new ground. You follow a script. Well, we're tired of it."

"Who's tired of it? You mean scientists?" I ask. "Without us, all this wouldn't even exist. We fund the space program."

"Yes, scientists are tired of you and your antics. And damn your ass, I know you fund it. But we're left out and it's not right. With this mission, we wanted to prove that scientists can be just as interesting, just as fun. So they prepared me and sent me. It took a lot of planning. I was the last person you suspected, wasn't I? Number two on the charts. Above all of you."

Everyone nods dumbly except me. I feel used. He got to show himself off by using me. And I totally fell for it.

I take a deep breath through my nose. I try to glare at him but the most I can manage is a pathetic grunt. I run a quick fist over my eyes.

"Weldon," he begins, voice going softer.

"Shut up. Don't ever call me by that name!" My hands are fists.

"So what were you going to do on this mission?" Darcy asks.

He scowls. "The ship's computers were going to malfunction, endanger the lives of us all. I would be the only one with the knowledge to save us."

"That's impossible." My voice is loud to my ears. Am I yelling? "The computers are controlled from Earth. If there's a malfunction, they fix it."

"I was to set it up so we'd plummet into Jupiter, into all that hydrogen and heavy gravity. The computers were to take more time to fix than we had. We'd break apart before control could be regained. So I was to take them off-line and pilot us out."

I frown because, you see, this is my ship and even I don't know how to fly her. "You know how to pilot this thing?"

"Yeah." Drac studies his lap.

"Wow," Armstrong says.

"What kind of scientist are you?" I ask.

"Astrophysicist. Pilot. Specialties…" He looks up. "The nature of stars and long-term spaceflight simulation."

"How come you never told me you were a scientist?" Danielle steps forward and bends to his level, glaring. "I'm your best friend."

"You became a Hero right out of school. You were never home. Left when I was still young. I never told you I went to another school for eight years after that because you wouldn't understand."

"You could have tried me," she protests.

He shakes his head. "Heroes are well-known for their prejudice toward scientists. So I never told you where I worked while you were gone in space. And, the typical self-centered Hero, you never asked."

"I thought you were a bum." Danielle reaches out to touch his cheek. "You always had money, though, so I thought mom and dad were helping you out."

Drac turns away.

"That's why I was so excited to help you out when you decided to become a Hero like the rest of the family. Why I'm here now. And you used me?" Danielle lets out a loud puff of air and stomps her foot.

Looks like Drac used everyone.

I feel that strange queasiness in my stomach again when I look at him. He really hates us.

The rest of my crew shifts uncomfortably. There's a brief silence.

"So, what are we going to do with him?" Armstrong scratches his left buttock and stares around the room.

"Let him go," I say.

Gasps fill the air. Only Danielle, Drac and I are silent.

"You can't let him go ahead with his plan," Hunter insists.

"He tried to kill you," Shariff says, crossing his arms.

"I wasn't trying to kill him. I thought he would kill *me*. I was trying to get the truth out of him!" Drac explains.

"Would you have killed me?" I ask.

"Would you have killed me if you'd known my plan?"

"Heroes don't kill except in self-defense. Besides, I've never killed anyone in my life. I'm a pacifist. But you should have already known that."

"I *was* defending myself," Drac says glancing at us all in turn. "When I saw you on the bridge with my file up, I thought you knew about me. I thought all of you knew." He looks imploringly at Danielle.

Danielle, kneeling at his feet, touches his bound hands. "And you think you're so smart," she whispers, brushing the hair back from his face.

She looks up at me. Drac follows her gaze. All of them are looking to me.

My heart is like broken glass in my chest. I have a decision to make.

Chapter Twelve

Space seems a lot blacker, the bulkheads a duller gray, when one of your crew is unhappy. And when your heart is broken into so many pieces you know you'll never find them all even if you have forever to search.

We voted to let Drac go. There were no hold-outs even though everyone seemed to want Drac dead. In truth, he seemed harmless enough. Would he still sabotage the ship? I made sure the answer would be no. I locked him out of every computer device on board.

I alerted our Earth-based computer techs to search for anomalous programs in our systems.

After that, we all watched Drac slink off in those seatless pants of his, go to his quarters and immediately switch on the privacy light.

No one's seen him since.

As a result, everyone's spirits decline. Hunter loses her appetite for fudge. Armstrong loses his for sex, and when I'm not feeling despondent over lost love, I feel guilty to have stolen the stars from someone who, in his own tedious, user-unfriendly way, might be as deserving as I.

This is a real life problem, and as the captain I'm obligated to solve it. I'm not liking it one bit. Problems are always best handled when you know the outcome beforehand. When they're scripted.

The morale on this ship sucks now. That's unscripted and I can't just wave my hand and un-do everything that's happened.

I consider paying Drac a personal visit, but I can't think of what we'd talk about now that I know we have nothing in common, that he's a scientist, that he doesn't really love me.

Still, we have over three months of our mission left and it will surely be a holo disaster if I can't get him to participate again in Hero activities. If I can't boost morale. Or stop my own private crying.

Since it's my responsibility to fix things, I decide I must learn everything about this new Drac to better understand the nature of his being. I've never known a scientist before.

My first step is to call up vids of him in action before our love affair began. I never wanted to spy on him before. Now it's all I seem to do.

I watch him in that first week on board when he stayed mostly to himself. When he does come out of his quarters, different crew members try to flirt or joke with him. There are many moments of him looking shocked or not amused. Stoic and untouchable. Strangely, it's unique and endearing. Almost innocent. Virginal. I guess I can see how fans might be intrigued, ask for more about him, tune in to see if he's showing more interest the next day and the next.

Certainly I bought the act. I was intrigued. So intrigued I fucking fell in love.

There are vids of him staring at the stars with the same fond look I remember him giving me. My eyes heat again. I blink hard and pull up more vids.

Alone all the time, he runs a few games in the playroom (he likes group interactive sports).

Even though he's alone ninety percent of the time, even I can see from the vids how photogenic he is, and how his looks and the way he moves engage the eye and the mind. He dominates every scene, even the most boring ones. He's got major Personality Charisma Factor, which is what the PTB looks for when signing us up.

After awhile of viewing his life habits, however, I notice an inquisitiveness in him that is not present in the others, including Danielle. Danielle is smart, but it's all book-learned. Drac figures things out, and he has a kind of curiosity that shows up at the oddest moments.

In one scene I watch him inspect a door frame, running his hands along the sloped angles. In another, he's got his ear cocked to the wall of the main engine unit, listening to who knows what. I've never heard a sound from our engines. The purr in the bulkheads is from the air turbos. In another vid, I watch him beat my live-mystery game in less than an hour.

My eyes burning, my brain filled to busting with Drac Drac Drac recordings, I decide to invite Danielle to my quarters for dinner. Because I know she will decline, I make it an order.

She stalks into my room wearing layers of black silk draped across her breasts, and long pieces of silk tied at the hip, leaving her midriff and right thigh bare. One piece she has used as a scarf to hide her hair.

"Why are you making me do this?" she grumbles as she goes to sit at the temporary table in the center of the room. She faces my port window to the stars.

"I want to talk about your brother."

"Please. I've been humiliated enough. Haven't you?"

It hurts but I ignore it. "I know. I'm sorry. But I have to know a few things. You know him best. He's your brother."

"But I don't want to talk about him," she says quietly. "I'm ashamed. And I feel betrayed."

"Were you really fooled by him?"

"Weren't you?" She plays with a thick gold bracelet on her forearm. It is the color of candlelight.

"Danielle, he's got great PCF, which might throw anyone off, but you had to notice certain things about him. His curiosity, for one."

"Yes." She shrugs, fingers the silverware. "And you had to notice it, too, after that long tour of the ship you gave him."

I pour us each a glass of white wine. She takes a slow sip before continuing. Her upper lip glistens.

"I thought he outgrew it," she begins. "He always experimented with things when we were kids. He made stuff like, you know, rocket ships and fireworks. Once he set the house on fire with some kind of new anti-gravity device he was trying to invent. It was just kid stuff, though, just a phase. He was so likeable, funny, you know, born to perform, and the rest of us just thought he was a natural-made Hero. Then he disappeared for awhile. He told me he was traveling the world. He wanted to see it all before he got older. I thought he was being a bum, you know, backpacking through the Himalayas or something."

"But he was lying."

"His whole life is a lie."

"Would you have accepted him if he told you the truth?" I ask.

Danielle looks up, blue eyes motionless in her star-lit face. "Yes."

"Is that the truth?"

She looks down. "I love him. I would have accepted it. Eventually."

I love him, too. Loved.

But is that past tense true? I have such strong feelings for him, even now. If I didn't feel so rejected…

I turn toward my viewport spacescape, sipping my wine. "We set ourselves up as superior."

"It's our job," she says.

"Yes, it's expected. We are, after all, Heroes. But sometimes I wonder who the real heroes are, with a small 'h'."

"People who brave the unknown, or do the impossible," she replies.

"And we don't really do that, do we?"

"No," she agrees. "I've come to realize that over the years. But we still serve a purpose. We keep the space industry going. We fund it. We make it fun and entertaining so people invest."

"That's the way it's always been, throughout history. You need flashy people or hype to sell things, even if those things are necessary, good for you, for the benefit of all Mankind. The real heroes never get the credit."

Danielle leans her chin on her upturned palm. Her eyes seek the view behind me and barely succeed in holding back a wave of shimmering tears. "How Drac must hate us."

*

I sit with the lights turned low in the mess hall. It's late ship's night. There should be tons of fucking going on, and happy people partying hard. The ship is way too quiet.

Despite the fact that Drac is not confined to his quarters, he hasn't come out for two days, not even for food.

Much as I don't know what to say to him, I feel obligated, as Captain, to schedule a visit.

I'm still mad. And hurt. More, I am afraid he really does hate us. Hate me.

The dinner with Danielle has given me some insight, but I'm still frustrated by my failure to see this coming. And my weakness for Drac. Facing Drac in my current mood is a disturbing prospect, and yet it seems he's starving himself in there, or performing some such dramatic gesture since he can't be starving. He has his Cokes and his frozen burritos.

I'm just about to the point of convincing myself to let him stay alone and call it a night, when Hunter bustles into the galley, her thick hair obscuring most of her face. The silver suit she wears clings so tightly from ankle to throat I wonder if her circulation is impaired.

"There you are," she announces to the room.

"I've been here for quite awhile," I point out. "What is it?"

"Sig's been tapping into Earth a lot, following the off-market charts. We thought you might want to know what we've just found."

"What?" Real dramatic tension is so different from pretend. Despite the pills Shariff gave me, my headache has returned.

"Drac's just gone to number one."

My mouth opens and freezes that way. I imagine I must look like a six-foot fish in pain.

"Not only that, it bumped John Luke to third."

Regaining my voice, I ask, "Well, then, who's second now?"

"You."

"Me?"

"It's upset the whole male listing. Apparently, someone got hold of the interrogation recordings and before the PTB could formally issue it, pirate copies got out. The civs love him. They love that he's a scientist." Her lips curl in a display of disgust. "They love that you stuck up for him."

"Great."

"I know. It's terrible, isn't it? The bastard has nice form in *danse l'amour*, a perfect PCF rating, and he's smart to boot! He didn't even need to save the ship to get votes." She harrumphs dejectedly and hops upon a nearby table, lying back. "He's ruining the competition. And now all the fans are dying to see you two make up."

The galley has the second largest viewport, rectangular and running the length of the room. The largest is on the observation deck. The bridge port takes third place in size.

From the angle of our ship right now, you can see Sol becoming more distant every day. Right now our star is the size of an apricot, and all that golden light pulsing at us makes Hunter, sheathed in silver, glow.

I get up and slowly approach her. "Ruining the competition?" I say. "No. It just spices it up."

She watches me hungrily. "Then let's compete." Already her hand has found the invisible seams of her suit. The pieces of it fall away from her like water, her voluptuous skin awash with stars.

"But I have to make up with Drac. You just said so yourself."

"Fuck, I don't understand all these stupid love stories the fans care about. Damn it! But I guess you're right. It'd be seen as cheating if you guys don't formally break up first before you fuck me." She stands naked before me, totally unself-conscious. I feel nothing.

It's Drac I want.

And I must go see him right now.

Chapter Thirteen

In my hand is a hot plate. Its contents include fettuccini alfredo and a frozen burrito I found in a large stash in the galley just in case he's run out of the ones in his personal freezer. Two meals from our first two dates. They mean a lot to me still.

I head straight for Drac's quarters.

Sigourney comes around a corner and raises both her dyed-white eyebrows. "My vote? Don't take him back. You should let him rot," she mutters, then moves past me in a scent of orchids.

I turn toward Drac's door. First I knock instead of hitting the buzzer. I expect no answer and have the override ready just in case — because I intend to see him one way or another — but after a mere two seconds the door slides open.

Drac's gaze moves from the plate in my hands to my face. "Well," he says, stepping away from the door to let me in. "You're the first. Not even my sister has visited me."

He doesn't look like hell, but he's got a tired slump. His face is paler, gaunt. He wears an ugly pair of shorts, red, which are baggy and show off nothing of his finer qualities. I see an old bag of dried chips on his bunk. It's empty.

"Been living on that?" I ask, nodding toward the bag.

He doesn't answer. He stands, arms folded, facing his desk. Amid a disarray of pillows, game headbands, boots, backless jeans and what look like real computer notebooks, I find a clear spot on the table by the couch and set down the plate. Just as I do, I see my lucky gold Sacagawea coin sitting in the center of the mess. I pick it up. It feels so cold, yet so familiar. I flip it twice across my knuckles.

Drac watches me. "Say what you came to say."

"Well," I begin. "I would, but I don't know *what* to say. I've never talked to a scientist before."

"Idiot," he mutters under his breath.

"I don't deserve that."

He turns to look at me. "No. You don't."

"What is your plan now? To just disappear from this mission? Lock yourself away for the next three months?"

He doesn't answer.

I go to his couch, sweep aside strewn pillows and clothing, and take a seat.

"The stars look pretty tonight, don't they?" I venture, gazing at his open viewport. He's turned up the colors and the magnification to include a rainbow effect. They are beautiful in this rendition.

His head bows; his arms unfold. I can see his fists clench. "We sleep the beauty of the night away, the dark wonder, secrets kept secret."

"What?"

He turns, grimacing. "Don't you recognize it? It's a poem *you* wrote."

"Oh. Yeah." I scrunch my right eye shut. "Wait. You have some of my poems memorized?"

"I thought you were writing about how too many people are not inquisitive, observant, aware. But you don't even remember writing it, do you?" Beneath a tangle of dark hair, his dark eyes glare.

"I've got tomes of that star-crap."

"I hate you," he says suddenly. He jerks himself back, away from me. His arms dangle back and forth as if he doesn't know what to do with them.

"Okay," I reply. "Now that we've got that out in the open…"

"You don't even try, do you? You don't even care."

I set the coin on the table. My hands rise, palms-up in question. "About what?"

"Everything. Anything."

"I care about you."

"Not sure about that," he replies in a low tone.

"You're wrong."

His head bows. He swings his hands forward again, clasps them in front of him. "You don't care why things are the way they are, what makes them work." He takes a step toward me.

"You mean science?"

He nods.

"I failed physics in school. Got a D in eleventh grade biology. I managed to skip chemistry altogether. Why would I pursue something I can't possibly understand?"

"Why pursue poetry?" he asks.

I stare at him. He's not trying to be funny, but I don't understand the question. "I just have words in my head banging to get out. That's all."

"Exactly."

I sigh loudly. "I don't get it."

"You love life. You love the stars. But what do you really know about either one? Why write about what you don't know?" He's starting to get passionate about the subject. I can tell by the stance of his body. And his eyes are more alert.

I'm beginning to get perturbed. "I'm not an intellectual like you."

"Says who?" He comes to stand in front of me.

"I'm no good at figuring things out. I saw you run that mystery game in less than an hour. I haven't gotten through it yet."

"I used to play it all the time in college. It took me a year to figure it out."

"Oh."

He waves my comment aside. "But that's not the point. Why pursue me? You didn't know me. In fact, I went out of my way to keep you from knowing me."

"I'll admit, it was shallow at first. You're my type. And I thought it might help my ratings."

"And then?"

"It did help my ratings." Hearing how that sounds, I add. "And then I just kept wanting to be around you."

"You thought you got to know me, but you found out I was a scientist and that was it. I'm last week's conquest."

"No—no. You're wrong." I lean forward, elbows on knees.

He continues to bombard me with questions. "Why does the PTB stress that knowledge is boring, that figuring out answers to real questions is low entertainment?"

"It doesn't rate well, that's a fact. And these missions cost money. They have to pay for themselves."

"It's because of media suggestion. Cultural programming. They don't make scientific exploration *exciting* enough. They play it down. There're fewer and fewer scientists because the media says it's drudgery to be one. And so nothing new is being done in space."

"Well, there you're wrong. This mission is a first. We're going to see if Jupiter has a core and what it's really made of. It might even make us all rich if we find diamonds or something."

He shakes his head, laughs. "Not diamonds. More like iron. Or gold. This mission isn't for furthering knowledge. It's a mining job. If the PTB get richer off it, maybe they won't need Heroes anymore and *your* job will be obsolete."

"It's still worth our while," I argue. "I have enough to retire anyway." But maybe there is never enough. With inflation, and how crazy Earth has become. I pause. "Gold, you say?"

He rolls his eyes. He does it often. Even in bed. I should feel insulted but I like it because it makes me know he's listening to me, maybe even taking me seriously. Even if I am an idiot.

"Well, how do you expect me to react?" I ask. "This is the biggest planet in the solar system. If it's a gold mine."

"At least you are starting to understand," he grumbles. "Space travel can pay for itself. It doesn't need—actors."

I pat the space on the couch next to me. "Sit down, Drac."

To my surprise, he does. I stiffen a little, still slightly intimidated by his smarts, but it gets easier with each passing minute. He's acting pretty Hero-ic, so it's getting easier to accept what he really is. A human being. A man with his own dreams even if they're not the same as mine. And he smells good. Like spice.

"Back home, for many years I was working on long-distance spaceflight. For trips outside the solar system."

"Really?" So hit me, it does sound intriguing.

"Yeah." After awhile, he hangs his head. The fringe of his long hair shadows his chest. "But that's not good enough. It seems nothing real is good enough for publicity unless it's sanctioned by the PTB."

"Well, that's not entirely true. We got distracted when I first came in here and there is something I wanted to tell you. Something you should know."

"What?" He sounds bored.

"It seems reality can be good enough as you put it. You're number one on the popularity charts, and you didn't land there until after it was discovered you were really a scientist."

His head comes up. His mouth is a perfect, dark 'O'. "Huh? Eh? Nah. Everyone believes scientists aren't sexy."

"Bullshit. Sexy is about trends. You're trending. And perhaps you always should have."

"Trending?" It's as if there's a light temporarily out in his eyes that's just clicked back on.

"You even beat me out: I'm number two."

The light in his eyes deepens. Dark depths sparkle. He leans toward me. "Really?"

"And you didn't even have to save us all from dying to get there."

"Really?" He grabs my shoulders, shakes me. "Really?"

"Yes." I try to shrug out of his grip but he's too strong. Instead, I just grunt.

"Really? I'm number one? Right now?"

"Yes. Yes! But it's crucial we play this right."

He turns toward me, knee bumping mine. "What do you mean play this right?"

"The fans are looking for some conclusion between you and me. Something—"

His eyelids lower. "I'm not going to play that game."

"It should be easy for you," I accuse. "You played me quite well this past week."

"Idiot."

"I believed you felt what I felt, damn it! So don't call me that. It's not fair." My voice goes gravelly on that last word. Tears smart in my eyes.

"No, I mean I wasn't playing you. It wasn't obvious?"

"You used me." I'm blinking fast.

He shakes his head. "I had no idea the ratings would go up. I was waiting for the computer malfunction. But you— you had nothing to do with all that. I didn't date you because of some stupid script."

"You didn't?"

He tilts his head, looking at me like I'm a child again. A look I'm quite familiar with. "Did you think I faked my orgasms?"

It takes me a moment to comprehend what he's just asked.

"Stirling," he says. "I'm not like you. I don't do casual. I got angry with you because I thought you knew about me being a scientist. I thought *you* used me!"

"I had no idea you weren't a Hero," I whisper.

Our eyes meet. I must look like some soap opera slut to the cameras. Tears on command. But these are real. I know it. And now Drac knows it, too.

Suddenly, he pulls me to him, kisses me hard on the lips. At first I'm in shock. I don't do anything. My hands are limp in my lap. My heart appears to have stopped.

After a few seconds, he pulls back. "Do you not want me anymore? Is it too much now? What I am?"

I look at him. He's beautiful, generous and kind. He's read—and memorized—my poems. He calls me by my real name when he comes. He's not an evil demon. He's not even a real criminal. He's just somebody who loves the stars. Like me.

"Drac," I say, knowing this is all being filmed and not caring. "I don't just want you. I love you."

"None of this—" he spreads his hands about us, "is fake. Reality *can* be better than fiction. I promise you, Weldon. I love you, too."

He's just said it. For real. He loves me, too.

Without any hesitation, I grab him by the shoulders and pull him back into the kiss.

This time I'm not stone. And my heart comes to life, hammering in my chest. Our lips burn as they meet and open. Instant connection is made. I want him. I need him. My cock goes quickly hard. My mind soars.

The next hour or so is like a dream. We embrace and fumble and struggle to touch each other deep, deeper. To some who have just tuned in, it might look like we're wrestling, or even downright fighting. But we are gripping, grabbing. We tear at each other's clothes.

"Damn," he says.

"Fuck," I reply.

We can't get close enough fast enough. He's hard as steel when I get my fingers around his cock. He thrusts into my grip.

I kiss him hard. My tongue meets his and tries to lock on. I pull back and dive for his throat, licking downward. I move across his chest, sucking in a nipple.

His hands fist in my hair, tugging. He falls back onto the couch with me between his legs. I press at his hips with my palms. My mouth goes to his stomach, licking, then I move down to the insides of his thighs, knowing that makes him crazy.

I suck the soft, nearly hairless skin there, making him buck and squirm.

By the time I reach his balls, they're tight and must be aching. My mouth leaves them wet and dripping.

I make him wait. I make him suffer. By the time I lick up the underside of his shaft he's throbbing hard and making pained noises that echo about the room.

I suck him down. It only takes a few bobs of my head before he comes hard. He pulls out, still shooting, and turns me over, but I guess he forgets we're not in bed. We both roll off the couch and fall onto the floor. Luckily, there are no injuries.

He grabs my cock and licks his way around it.

Before I know it, I'm coming down his throat.

We don't stop there. The lovemaking doesn't end. We stroke and caress until we're ready again.

At one point, when we are coming down from another orgasmic high, Drac jumps up and starts dancing and hopping around the room like a deranged psychotic. "I'm number one," he says to himself, repeating it over and over. It becomes a song. "I'm number one."

"You're rating is going to fall rapidly if you don't stop that soon." But I'm laughing hard enough from where I'm sitting naked on the floor to make my stomach ache.

He turns. His grin is all I need to see to make me realize my words are wrong.

Drac doesn't need to *do* anything. No daring rescue attempts, no circus spacewalks, no acting, he just exudes natural Hero-ism. He's what the PTB has been looking for for decades without ever knowing it.

Hunter is right. The competition will never be the same. PCF, brains, looks, sexual prowess, he's got it all. None of us Heroes are a match. And, I fear, by the end of this scene our world as we know it will never be the same.

Epilogue

There are portions of our desperate lovemaking session that night we made up that to this day remain blank. I was in a dream, a fog of such love and craving and acute arousal that reality slipped away as easily as light on an event horizon.

Days later, I cannot bring myself to watch the vid, though it topped the charts as soon as the producers could get it out to the masses. I never watch myself perform on the vids. I thought this time I might make an exception. But every time I think I'll take a peek, I turn away.

Drac tells me with a grin, "Why watch a holo when you have the real thing?"

And he's right. I do have the real thing.

Today we're on the bridge, staring outward through the viewport. He's set the magnification so the stars are like Christmas tree lights in the night. The stars are like eyes, I think, little bursts of wisdom, of beauty. We are but shadows in their bloom.

"How could you ever love those lights in the sky and not yearn to know what they're called, how they speak, what they're made of?" He leans back in the captain's gold chair — my chair, damn him — and his eyes flash with the intimacy of knowledge and wonder.

I'm ready for it now, ready for words and numbers and tongue-tangling theories. I've got the right teacher. And I've got time. Besides, the projected returns on this recording tentatively titles *Science Lessons 101* promise to beat out all the past top holo hits combined."

"All right, Drac," I say, watching the ancient light play in his black hair. I lean against the armrest, the closest I'll get anymore to my chair until I've earned it. The first step is always the hardest. "Teach me."

I stare at where the gold mesh of his tank breaks away to reveal the taut muscles of his chest. Then, with an effort, I glance up and out to the undying universe. "Begin with the texture of stars."

the end

Contact links for Wendy Rathbone:

Join my Facebook group Wendyland. I post updates, cover reveals, snippets, sales and other fun stuff every day: https://www.facebook.com/groups/718074255203918/

Facebook: https://www.facebook.com/wendy.rathbone.3

Newsletter sign up (you get a free copy of my contemporary mm romance *The Bodyguard's Valentine*): https://claims.prolificworks.com/free/k5uTgYuU

Amazon author page: https://www.amazon.com/Wendy-Rathbone/e/B00B0O9BMS/ref=dp_byline_cont_ebooks_1

Dear Reader:

Thank you for reading *Not Another Hero.*

Please consider leaving a review. Word of mouth is like gold! If it weren't for the generous support of my readers, I could not be writing more books!

You might also enjoy subscribing to my newsletter. I put it out several times a year to announce new books and upcoming projects, and I always have sales and freebies to offer readers both from myself and other authors I enjoy reading. If you subscribe at the link below, you can get a free copy of my contemporary mm romance **The Bodyguard's Valentine.**

Or, if newsletters aren't your thing, it is very easy to sign up for my Facebook group Wendyland to keep up to date. I am there almost every day, and I post current updates all the time.

For new release notifications, it's also super easy to simply follow my author page on Amazon.

Happy Reading!

Love,

Wendy Rathbone

About Wendy Rathbone

Read Wendy Rathbone… where imposters and outcasts, princes and lost boys always find their happily every after.

I have written in all genres: sci-fi, fantasy, horror, paranormal, contemporary, erotica, romance. But I keep coming back to romance as the main focus. Gay romance. Male/male romance. The idea of two men falling in love is irresistible to me. It's all I write now.

All my books are available on Amazon and most are in Kindle Unlimited. So if you have the urge, go take a look. See what's on the shelf.

Love to you all!

Wendy Rathbone

THE SLAVE HAREM
Wendy Rathbone

The slave harem is all. If you enter, you can never leave. Contact with the outside world is forbidden.

With a secret talent for seeing auras of physical and emotional arousal, Ren, a sought-after pleasure slave, is sold to a mysterious master in a foreign land where he will become part of a collection of beautiful men.

Though the men appear welcoming, there is competition and jealousy among the ranks. And their mysterious master who is heard but never seen elicits more questions than answers.

One friendly slave, Li Po, helps Ren settle in, but it is the voiceless man, Zanti, who draws Ren's attention. With his wicked beauty and bratty scowls, Zanti is the least welcoming of them all, and Ren's training and control are put to the test.

Gay harem, slow-burn, enemies to lovers. Extraordinary and strange. Hot and cold. This book explores the many levels of sex, lust, loneliness and belonging. And maybe, just maybe, there can be love.

THE SLAVE PALACE
Wulf and Locke
WENDY RATHBONE

Conquered. Captured. Sold as a pleasure slave.

After being taken as a prisoner of war, Wulf fights his captors and is sold as a One-Night Thrall to be used and abused, then put to death. He is purchased by a high ranking master of the famous Slave Palace. Why Locke buys him, Wulf has no clue, but something about this master is intriguing. Instead of abuse, Wulf is plied with luxuries he has never known by a man who actually seems to respect him.

Jaded. Looking for a challenge.

Eminent Master Locke takes on a bet with his best friend that he can't train and tame a dangerous One-Night Thrall in ten days. But something about this slave stirs him like no other before. All bets aside, Locke has the urge to keep Wulf, as well as save his life. But Wulf is fierce, unwilling, and his consent papers have been forged. If Wulf doesn't soon submit to his role as a slave, he will be sent to death as a prisoner of war.

A sweet, slow-burn love story taking place on an alternate contemporary Earth where owning pleasure slaves is legal.

LORD VAMPYRE
Wendy Rathbone

When Lord Neverelle becomes a guest at Cliffside Keep, Vanni watches helplessly as Damion, the young man he's grown up with and secretly loves, falls for the alluring and seductive stranger. Lord Neverelle is danger incarnate, and soon takes control of the household.

Not satisfied with Damion alone, Never uses a vampire trick called "the tempt" to compel Vanni, who is swept into a love triangle that includes fiery passion and nightly threesomes.

Now Vanni must ask himself, is any of this consensual? And what about Damion—does he really want to be with Vanni, or is it all a sensual play controlled by vampire compulsion?

M/M and M/M/M romance.

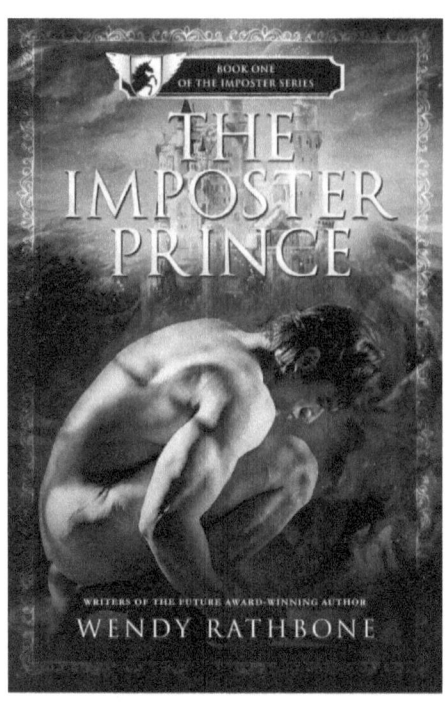

The Imposter Prince
Book 1 in The Imposter Series
Wendy Rathbone

His love for an enemy prince threatens his very life.

Dare does not mind serving the spoiled and cruel Prince Darius. Growing up with him, Dare does everything for Darius including homework, bed play demands, and even doubling for him as the prince grows too paranoid to face even the smallest of crowds.

But everything changes in a single moment when Dare, while posing as Darius, is abducted by the enemy.

A captive in a new and hostile land, Dare meets another prince who seems just as indulged and rotten as Darius—until Dare gets to know him, until they fall in love. Against his will, Dare must continue to play the role of Prince Darius for real, or risk everything: his love, his land, and his very life.

His only chance for survival is to keep a secret from the one he loves, a secret that is also killing him.

A male/male, enemies to lovers novel of mad kings, troubled princes, abduction, fevers, cold dungeons, warm hearths, comfort, wine, and true love.

THE IMPOSTER KING
(Book 2 of The Imposter Series)
Wendy Rathbone

Their love made them close.
Their secret kept them closer.

Dare and Prince Malory are happily married and in love, but the secret of Dare's true identity as a mere servant threatens their romantic bliss.

Messages to the king of Brookfall go unanswered, and rumors of war unsettle both kingdoms. Until one day heralds arrive with bags of gold to ransom Dare and demand his return to Brookfall.

King Millard, Prince Malory's father, orders Dare to make the journey to see his father. But Dare is not the true heir, and if they meet, the secret he and Mal have been guarding will be revealed. Also, impersonating a royal means a death penalty offense. Worse, it could mean all-out war between their countries.

Panic. Despair. Lovers torn asunder. Personal sacrifice. More dark secrets revealed. An ending that will leave you breathless.

Ganymede: Abducted by the Gods
Book 1 in "The Fantastic Immortals" Series (A standalone read)
Wendy Rathbone

My name is Ganymede, and I have been betrayed.

Every boy my age dreams of leaving home to embark on a noble adventure, but never does any boy imagine it happening as it did to me. On the evening of my 18th naming day, when I expected no more than a chalice of wine and a few drunken flirtations to tempt my innocence, I was instead sold by my father to the god, Zeus - not because of anything particular I had ever done or said, but solely because I am considered beautiful among mortals, and my father found more value in a few gold coins than in the well-being of his youngest son.

To be honest, I never believed in the gods, but my lack of belief held no power in Olympus or on Earth. Now under Zeus's influence, I am kept drunk on ambrosia in the sun-lit halls of the immortals, alternately amazed and horrified at the power these beings hold over others, and how darkly they influence the progress of humanity itself. How very much I want to hate Zeus for kidnapping me, and yet he shows me mostly kindness, even on that fateful night when we shared a bed for the first time. Kindness, yes, but also a godly and unyielding refusal to take no for an answer... probably because he could read my ambrosia-fevered curiosity as much as my naive, inexperienced terror. He owns me, after all, just as he owns everything else, so perhaps it never occurred to him that a captive and a slave might not make the best of lovers.

Throughout my time at Olympus - who's to say how long I've been here, for time on Olympus is not the same as that on Earth - the only thing that gives me hope comes to me in dreams and visions. His name is Sable and he is a magnificent shape-shifter in the form of a giant raven. When he first spoke to me in my mind it was with a resonance unlike any I had ever known - his mind and mine sounding a single note together, a song without words, a promise of freedom, a glimpse of some distant but very real possibility of this thing we humans call Love. But now he is silent. Perhaps I dreamed his voice. Perhaps I have finally lost my mind.

ZEUS (Conquering His Heart)
Book 2 in "The Fantastic Immortals" Series (A standalone read)
WENDY RATHBONE

When I throw the lightning and summon the thunder, it isn't always out of anger, but often from a love so all-consuming it could only be the effect of Eros himself. Yes, he is beautiful. Of course he is. How could he be otherwise, with hair the color of sunlight and white-feathered wings that drape to the floor? And he is as ancient as the myth of time itself, an immortal with powers and glamour beyond my ability to imagine. He struggles to teach me wisdom, control, strategy, yet I sit here babbling like a child, for all I can think of is how I might try - at least let me try! - to prove myself to him in some way that will cause him to crave my company and my touch, just as I crave his.

I do not yet know how to be a god, for I am only 18 and still just a silly boy who has fallen in love with Love himself, while my father Cronus plots and schemes to lock me in his dungeon and make me his slave forever.

A male/male romance.

BUYING YOU
Wendy Rathbone

It's one thing to be a beautiful cover model on billboards, buses and magazine covers. It's quite another to be sold as one.

Prized for his looks, Dane knows it's shallow, but he is on his way to having it all. It feels good to be gorgeous, smart and have top designers from around the world requesting him.

When he returns to his hometown to participate in a small Date-For-Charity auction, it seems harmless enough—until a hooded man walks in and bids higher on him than anyone else. Dane is intrigued but nervous when he finds out the guy has vanished after the winning bid, leaving only a limo behind to whisk Dane off into the night.

Enemies to lovers, opposites attract, and hot steamy nights that challenge two guys' trust issues along with their biggest fears.

The Foundling, Rescue Me (Book 1)

What do you do when you find an unconscious man floating on a raft in the middle of the Caribbean? Rescue and fall in love with him, of course!

Well, that's not me! I'm a businessman first and foremost with an underworld reach that stretches from my island all the way to Miami. I'm too busy to rescue strays. I have no time for lovers. And I don't fall in love.

But Alec is beautiful, vulnerable, and my heart won't stop pounding. My every waking thought is of him. I can't concentrate. The world is suddenly vibrant and colorful. Flowers assault me with their sweet fragrance. Food tastes fresher. And my body is hot, so hot all the time.

I have done some dark deeds in my life and cared little for their affects on others as long as they gained me everything I sought. But now… one good deed and I don't know who I am anymore.

Billionaire, organized crime, amnesia, hurt/comfort, tropical hot-hot, happy for now. Book one of the Foundling trilogy. (Previously published under the title "The Foundling," this book is a newly edited, updated edition.)

The Foundling, Sacrifice Me (Book 2)
What do you do when your beautiful new lover's life is in danger and he wants to be bait to catch the enemy? You protect him with all your might.

Alec is still trying to remember who he is and is haunted by terrible nightmares. Diego is being investigated for murder. Their chemistry grows hotter and stronger even as Diego's ex, Sasha, comes for a visit and looking for a job.

Who can they trust to help them? Enemies are everywhere and the jungle closes in.

The Foundling, Remember Me (Book 3)

What do you do when your memories return and the most horrific nightmare you can imagine is real?

You try to bury it. You try to run. But none of that works.

Your lover is rock solid. He is always there for you, but is it enough?

Diego and Alec now live under witsec in San Francisco, thousands of miles away from the Caribbean. But their past still haunts them.

Alec is beginning to remember who he really is, but reliving the torment he went through threatens to destroy his sanity. Is Diego's love enough to hold onto such a broken man?

SONS OF NEVERLAND
Della Van Hise

Set against a backdrop of contemporary culture, *Sons of Neverland* explores the universal questions of love, sex and death - the three most crucial challenges every human being must face. Stefan London is a grieving man, suffering through the loss of his young daughter. When he goes to a science fiction convention in the hopes of meeting her friends, he encounters instead a man who is dangerously seductive. Lured into the night, Stefan soon discovers himself in a world where vampires are real, and immortality is only a kiss away.

But the price of eternal life is high, and as his handsome maker warns, "Through my blood you will learn a secret that will compel you to live forever, yet a secret so sinister it will haunt you for that same eternity."

The secret will haunt you, too.

***

One Reviewer said...
"Sons of Neverland" brings the reader face to face with the possibility that nothing we have been told by teachers, peers and priests holds a single gram of truth. The book is told in the poetic voice of myth, from the perspective of a man devastated by grief. As the story unfolds, Stefan's faith is not only tested, but destroyed - leaving him devastated but simultaneously free for the first time in his life... daring to stare love in the face of an immortal vampire."

Readers have compared this male/male romance to the works of Anne Rice and Anais Nin.

Eye Scry Publications
A Visionary Publishing Company
www.eyescrypublications.com